Let me
show you

LET ME SHOW YOU

BECCA SEYMOUR

For information, contact the author:
authorbeccaseymour@gmail.com

Editing: Hot Tree Editing

Cover Designer: BookSmith Design

Publisher: Rainbow Tree Publishing

E-book ISBN: 978-1-925853-49-0

Paperback ISBN: 978-1-925853-68-1

Surround yourselves with beautiful souls and the rest will fall in to place.

Liv, this one's for you.

CHAPTER ONE

CARTER

I CRACKED MY NECK AND THE TENSION GAVE WAY. IT had been a long day. Between an emergency surgery, back-to-back appointments, and barely time to inhale my caffeine hit let alone chew my sandwich, I was ready to head home.

I looked around my consultation room, ensuring everything was in place. While the cleaning staff would be by after the clinic closed, I still had a particular way of setting up my space. Lauren always laughed about me being anal-retentive, but I was far from it. Okay, admittedly not that far from it. I was just organized and liked everything in order.

I closed the door behind me as I entered the small hallway that led to the reception area just as the woman who liked to tease my ass stepped out of another room. "Hey, you heading home too?"

She pulled the door closed and smiled. "Yep. It's been a long day." She wasn't wrong. We'd both come in for the emergency surgery at four that morning after receiving a call from a distraught dog owner. Her pet Labrador had eaten a sock, so she'd rushed him in. His intestine was unsurprisingly inflamed and close to rupturing, so I'd had to perform abdominal surgery to remove the blockage.

Having Lauren by my side giving me a helping hand made the morning go that much faster, and more importantly, as the best nurse on staff—not that I was biased or anything since she was my friend—it meant that the surgery went perfectly. It was a huge relief. It also meant that I was ready to pick up some food, as I was too bone-tired to cook, and then head home to eat before collapsing in bed.

We walked out together, waving and saying goodbye to a few more staff milling around. I yawned as I reached the car. "Geez, I feel like just crawling inside and sleeping in the car."

Lauren snorted. "I get it, but get your cute ass to bed. If not, you'll look like crap tomorrow."

I grunted. It hardly mattered these days if I looked crappy or not. There was no one to look good for, no one to appreciate any effort I might make. Heck, even shaving seemed like a chore. Life outside work had been nothing but stale and admittedly nonexistent since moving to town six months earlier. I couldn't see that changing anytime soon.

She threw me a wink when I rolled my eyes. "What?" she added.

I shook my head in answer.

She grinned, seeming to understand my silence when she wriggled her brows and she said, "You never know, there could be a sex god just waiting around the corner to sweep you off your feet." She paused at my look of disbelief. It seemed she'd read my "as if that would ever happen" expression. "Stranger things have happened."

I scoffed, a genuine smile chasing it. "Here, in this town?"

She pursed her lips as if considering her response. When she didn't say anything, I answered for her. "Yeah, thought not. If you hadn't noticed, there's hardly a line of guys walking around the place waving the rainbow flag."

It was Lauren's turn to roll her eyes at me. "Well, with that attitude—"

I laughed. "Honestly, Lauren, it's nothing about attitude. It's the reality of the town." I shrugged as nonchalantly as possible. "And that's okay. Most of the people are... nice." And they were. The rumor mill had churned about my move and appointment to the local veterinary clinic, but I was relieved that my sexuality, while often spoken about in hushed whispers, hadn't impacted on my work or standing in the community.

It sounded ridiculous even thinking that. I'd relocated from a city, and from a strong and large gay community. Acceptance had become my norm, even though that hadn't always been the way. But my new reality was Kirkby. It was only a small town of about eight thousand. It was a place where people tended to know everyone else's business. They damn well knew all about me, my late grandfather whose house I'd inherited, my sexuality, and I wouldn't have been surprised if they knew my exact height, weight, and social security number.

Lauren considered me a moment, not quite convinced I was being honest with her or myself. Admittedly, I wasn't quite convinced either. Maybe me being at peace with my place in town, my bachelor status that I didn't envision changing anytime soon, was a more accurate explanation of how I felt. "Hmm... well, I'll see you tomorrow. We'll also head out for a drink soon." She blew me a kiss and then headed toward her car. "Bye." She waved her hand above her head.

I watched her go and called out, "Good night." When she was behind her steering wheel, door closed and engine running, I got in my car and made my way to the pizza place. Another night with pizza for one. I sighed. At least it would give me leftovers for lunch tomorrow.

CHAPTER TWO

TANNER

It hadn't been an easy move, though it was one of necessity. Work was slowly picking up, which was a huge relief, but it didn't quite extinguish the flicker of anxiety that would light in my chest whenever I thought of the added responsibilities on my shoulders. I had to make this move a success.

It was easy over the years to be a selfish prick. Having only myself to look out for meant I could go anywhere I wanted, be anyone I wanted, and happily do anyone I wanted. It meant the last three months had been a huge fucking shock to my system.

I was still at that difficult impasse of having guilt gnawing my stomach whenever I wished I was anywhere but here, yet never regretting for one moment my decision to head to Kirkby.

I looked around at the white picket fences and the tree-lined street I was pulling out of. I begrudgingly understood why Davis had chosen to relocate and stay in such a town. It was quaint and full of the sort of charm that evolved naturally over generations of families looking after the place and having a community that stood together.

It was one thing I'd noticed since making the decision to relocate permanently, after I'd realized just how much Davis was struggling. The whole community had rallied around him, offering what I was sure was genuine support and honest murmurs of regret. But I'd known that Davis needed family, and it just so happened that I was it. While we weren't technically brothers, Davis had been my best friend since we were four and we were as close as brothers could be. We'd been through everything together, so with this new twist in his life, there was no way I would abandon him. We were the only family we had left, along with the recent addition of my niece.

So I'd packed up my business, put my house on the market, and headed out to offer what support I could. I wasn't quite convinced about what help I was actually giving, as what the fuck did I know about babies, other than they screamed, slept, and shit? Literally the three s's. But still, I tried and had since taken the additional responsibility of being Davis's only support system.

I stopped at the crossroad and eyed the bar at the corner, but thought better of it. Davis would be crapping bricks if I didn't get back. Libby was teething, so I knew she was having difficulty sleeping and was keeping them both up at night. Snorting, I shook my head as I pulled out safely and continued to Davis's. At some point over the past three months we'd created this whole new domestic routine. It involved a huge amount of tag-teaming, not only for helping out whenever I could with Libby, but for making sure I gave him a break after I'd finished work. That and being his shoulder when he thought he'd lose his mind. It worked. Now.

When I'd first moved, I'd made the mistake of living with him and Libby. As much as I loved them both, it was far too fucking much like domestic bliss, without the added benefit of banging someone I loved or having a partner who was a tidy fucker. It had been years since Davis and I had shared space. We'd lived together after school and had made it work. Things had seriously changed since then. Back in the day, we'd been out virtually all the time, usually partying and fucking. We hadn't cared if the place was tidy, or if the laundry or dishes were done. Our new situation was so different, and since we'd quickly discovered that, I'd taken on a rental just a block away so I was able to step in as a good brother and favorite uncle rather than something that had been too close to husband for my liking.

After pulling up on Davis's drive, I switched off the engine and hopped out. I pushed the front door open, knowing it would be unlocked. Not only was it *that* sort of neighborhood where the neighbors would stop by with baked goods, but it was a really safe town. I didn't call out as I checked the time on my watch, trying to figure out if Libby would already be in the bath or not. A gurgle followed by a small laugh drifted to me from the kitchen/dining room. I smiled at the sound. Libby was a fucking angel—well, until she was armed with a spoon and her mushed-up food.

"Libby, come on, baby girl, open wide for Daddy." A clank and curse followed. "You did not just do that."

A grin stretched my mouth as I headed toward the sound. "What's for dinner?" I stepped into the space and found Libby looking thoroughly happy with herself as she banged a spoon on her high chair, orange baby food flying everywhere. Her big brown eyes landed on me and she gurgled in delight. Damn straight, she loved her some Uncle Tanner. Understandable. My eyes then landed on Davis and loud laughter burst from my mouth. There was orange goo on the top of his head, smeared across his cheek, and a glob hanging from his nose.

"Perfect timing," Davis grumbled. He stood, placed a kiss on his daughter's head, and headed toward me. Before I knew it, I was armed with a spoon and a bowl of Libby's ammunition, and watching Davis hightail it out of the room. "Off to grab a shower. Good luck!" he shouted over his shoulder.

"Right." With my brows lifted in amusement, I scrunched my nose at Libby and poked out my tongue. She giggled, banging her spoon some more. "You getting at your daddy again, huh, sweetheart? Just you wait till you're a bit older. I'll give you so many ideas about how you can really wind him up." Settling down in front of her, I continued to pull faces. She opened her mouth with glee, so I took the opportunity and shoveled in a mouthful of food. Yeah, I was definitely her favorite. She slapped her gummy mouth happily and made little noises of contentment before opening for another.

Okay, I was pretty good at this uncle shit after all.

———

I CRACKED OPEN TWO BEERS AND SETTLED DOWN IN the chair, waiting for Davis to return from putting Libby to bed. After feeding her and having some playtime while I gave Davis some time out, I'd offered to put her to bed, but I'd known Davis would take over. He'd admitted to me already it was one of his favorite times of the day with her.

At the time I'd laughed and asked if it was because she would be asleep and he'd have the night to unwind. He'd actually looked offended, and it hadn't taken long in the one month I'd stayed under his roof to see the attraction of bedtime snuggles with Libby. There was something surprisingly calming about her soft coos and gentle yawns that followed her fun bath time.

I heard the creak of the staircase as Davis made his way down. Taking a pull of my beer, I looked at the open door and gave him a chin lift when he entered. "All good?"

With a smile, Davis nodded. "Yeah, out like a light."

I bobbed my head. "She seems to be settled again. That's good." For a week now, Libby had attended a childcare place a few blocks away so Davis could return to work. He'd stayed at home looking after her since the day she was born, and while the two of us had made the process of finding a childcare facility or nanny a nightmare since we'd run it like a military operation, six months at home being a stay-at-home dad had finally taken its toll. Davis loved Libby something fierce... we both did, but Davis had been going stir-crazy not working.

Finally, after a week of settling into a new routine, it seemed both Libby and Davis had chilled the fuck out. Christ, I'd been the calm, levelheaded one over the past week as I'd caught Davis twice scoping out the childcare place during the day when he should have been working. I'd even caught him looking at the website to purchase one of those nanny cam things. I'd had to talk him down and be all responsible and shit. And that was a fucking feat in itself. I wasn't really known for keeping my temper in check.

He picked up his beer with a thanks, took a gulp, and asked, "How's work?"

"Good. Same old stuff. Though I'm off to price a job tomorrow. Looks promising and a big job. It would be nice to secure something that took longer than a few days or a week, you know?"

He nodded as he sat opposite me on the sofa.

"Yeah." He rubbed a hand over his face and yawned. "I get it."

Davis owned a coffee shop in town. He was actually a trained chef and had worked at a couple of high-starred restaurants in the city. His world had spun and changed so much though when a one-night stand had turned into a pregnancy, the result being Libby.

Mags, Libby's mom, was something of a free spirit and had been born and raised in Kirkby. It was how Davis had ended up here. He'd bought a small café that now did great coffee, and he'd turned his years of cooking into the job of pastry chef. He'd given the town plenty to gossip about as well as celebrate. He was a fucking good baker. It meant that the café was always busy, locals and tourists desperate for decent coffee and kickass cakes and pastries.

The gossip came in the form of Mags up and leaving the day after she'd given birth to Libby. While the town had been left speculating and filled with horror, Davis hadn't. I'd known he and Mags had discussed her leaving when she'd been pregnant, and Davis had happily agreed that he'd raise Libby. After their one night together, they'd never actually been together again, nor were they ever a couple.

The whole thing was freakin' weird, but then, to each their own.

To be honest, I was kind of relieved. Mags was a bit of a space cadet, and I hadn't been convinced she and Davis would have balanced the shared-parenting gig well. Hell, I definitely never imagined him dating her. While Davis had dated a few times over the years, and had once had a steady girlfriend, he tended to be with guys more often than not. I could definitely relate to the need for a hard body rather than squishy breasts, but Davis was a lover of all forms and packages. It was clear, though, a few weeks into being a new single dad that Davis was struggling, and yeah, the rest was history.

"Is the job in town?"

"Yeah," I answered. "Just the other side of town." I was looking forward to checking it out. Over the years my trade had grown from that of carpenter, to builder, plasterer, and even plumber on occasion. It meant I'd been able to pick up work quite quickly trading under my own name, but I was over fitting wardrobes and new doors, plastering a wall or two. I was eager for a project I could sink my teeth into. "I'll head by after securing the new garage door over on East Street." I drained my beer and looked at the time. "You need anything before I get going?"

"Nope. I'm good, thanks." Davis stood and walked me out, giving me a squeeze on my shoulder. "Have a good night."

I laughed. "Yep. Me, a beer, some oil, and my hand. Living the dream, man." I stepped out and headed to my truck.

He snorted. "That makes two of us. You seriously need to get laid so I can live vicariously through you, Tanner. Damn, dude, you're letting me down."

I snorted right back as I pulled open the door. "Yeah sure. I'll get right to that. Just point out the local gay bar and I'm all over it."

His laughter chased me into the car. I returned his wave and backed out of the drive, wishing I wasn't thinking about getting laid. Maybe it was time for a weekend away. Desperate times and an overused hand called for long-ass journeys into the city.

CHAPTER THREE

CARTER

WORK HAD BEEN MUCH CALMER, WITH NO emergencies and a shorter day. My job was pretty awesome. Not only because I was a veterinarian—what wasn't there to love about that?—but while I worked full-time at the practice, the hours were quite forgiving. A couple of longer shifts, plus being on call, meant I had three days a week of finishing by two.

It felt like I had the possibility of having a life. The only problem was, outside of Lauren, my friendship group was narrow. But still, I'd known when I'd moved that I'd be starting fresh, coming in with nothing apart from the home my grandfather had left me and a desire to make it work.

Looking around the dilapidated house, it wasn't

the first time I questioned my sanity. The house was in a bad state of disrepair, though I sucked it up and saw it as my penance for being a not so great grandson the past few years before my granddad died. It wasn't that we'd argued or anything. It was just, heck, I'd been young and busy, not only with studying and then work, but trying to get a life.

It hadn't helped that he always chose to ignore my sexuality and would send me links to straight porn and try to hook me up with local girls during the rare visits I made. The day when I'd first received an e-mail from my grandad, I'd been as impressed as I was confused. He'd always hated technology. Later my dad had told me he'd hooked him up with Wi-Fi and a laptop. I had no idea though how he'd been introduced to the many weird porn sites he'd discovered.

He'd been a character for sure. And while at the time he'd infuriated the heck out of me, point-blank refusing to believe I liked men and that no matter how hard he tried to convert me, a vagina would make me gag and run screaming in the opposite direction, I'd still loved the stubborn old fool.

When Dad had told me about the will, I'd been dumbfounded. It was Mom who'd smiled lovingly at me and suggested I check out the house and give some serious thought about where I wanted to be, where I saw my life heading.

It wasn't like I had been living life to any level of extreme, nor was I lonely, but I was finally honest with myself and recognized I'd been in a rut.

Looking around my new home, I shook my head, not quite sure I was any better off.

My cell rang. I headed to the kitchen and picked it up from where it had been charging.

Looking at the caller ID, I greeted, "Hey, Mom."

"Hey, baby boy." I smiled. In my late twenties, I was far from a baby, but she'd once told me that even at fifty I'd still be her baby. "Good day?"

"Yep. Not too bad. Nothing too hectic or crazy. You?"

"A great one. Your dad's booked a cruise for our anniversary." Excitement lit her words. She'd been hinting at Dad for a while about a cruise. I was pleased he'd listened. It didn't take a lot to make my mom happy; she found joy in the smallest of things, so that he'd organized it all was pretty impressive. Mom usually organized everything, so I knew him booking the vacation for them was a big deal.

"That's terrific. Caribbean?"

She actually squealed down the line. I pulled the

phone from my ear and laughed loudly. "Yes! Carter, I'm so excited."

"Really? I'd never have guessed."

"Oh, hush." She spoke over me as I laughed again. "Don't sass your mother."

My laughter continued. "Never, Mom. You'd tan my hide. Wouldn't dream of it."

"I should think not. So anything new? Any dates?"

With a groan, I rubbed my face and then stepped further into the kitchen and pulled out a glass. "Mom...," I sighed.

"What? I worry about you. You're so far from home and are there all alone."

I poured myself a glass of wine and took a sip. "I know you worry, but honestly, life's good." Admittedly it would have been nice to hook up, but one, I didn't do casual and never had, and two, there was no way I'd tell my mom I was afraid my penis would drop off from lack of use. "There's nothing new either, and that's okay. I'm liking the quiet life."

"Hmm...." That was her tell for not being convinced. "You know, I was talking to Julie last week, and her nephew's gay."

"Mom," I said with laughter, "honestly, no hookups. I do not need my mom fixing me up."

She ignored me. "Well, he lives quite far away, but maybe a week of casual—" She cleared her throat. "—sex would do you good."

"Jesus, Mom." I spluttered on my mouthful of wine. Grabbing a towel, I wiped my face, catching the dribble of red wine on my chin, and wiped the countertop I'd sprayed. "Stop. I don't need you arranging anything, okay? Please tell me you're listening." She was quiet. "Mom," I said louder.

"Yes, yes, I hear you." She sighed. "Grandbabies would be nice."

Holy crap on toast! With wide eyes, I looked at the ceiling and counted to five. I then took a big gulp of wine before saying, "Mom."

"Yes, baby boy?"

"I have to go. I need to grab a shower. I'm expecting someone."

"Ooh—"

"Someone to fix the house up." I'd heard the interest in her tone, the hope in that one syllable.

"Oh." This time her voice dropped. I hated to kill her enthusiasm, but geez, I really needed to get off the phone.

"Love you, tell Dad I love him too. And I'll speak to you guys later. Bye, Mom."

"Will do." Her tone was a bit brighter. "Love you

too. Bye, honey."

I disconnected quickly and placed my phone down. My mom, yeah, she was wonderful and drove me to absolute distraction. I knew how lucky I was. Every decision I'd ever made, my parents had always had my back. They supported me unconditionally. It was just that my mom could be a little extreme at times. I laughed into the empty room. I wouldn't have it any other way.

Quickly finishing my wine, I looked at the time. I had just fifteen minutes until the contractor was due. I'd left it late to organize myself, still a little in a tizz after the conversation with my mom and the mention of babies. I glanced around the room at the disorderly mess. Every time I did so, I regretted it.

I detested chaos, and that was what the house felt like. The place was still strewn with my moving boxes, but I had yet to see the point in unpacking. Not necessarily because I planned to move, but rather, the whole house needed a lot of work, so I knew I'd have to pack my things up for any work on the house to start.

I really hoped this Tanner guy would be the person who could finally help me out. I'd had two other quotes, one local and one from out of town. Both were crazy high, and neither would be able to start for another five months or so. I was running out of options. This guy had come recommended to me by one of my clients, but I didn't want to get my hopes up.

I sighed in defeat as I looked around. I'd have to continue ignoring it all until I finally had the place fixed up. I headed upstairs, careful to miss the couple of steps that had loose boards, and headed to the main bathroom. I had an en suite, but the shower didn't work, so it was the pearlescent green suite I headed toward. The sickly porcelain made me shudder every time I laid eyes on it. It was clean though, so there was that.

I hopped into the shower, lathered myself up, and quickly rinsed off. That was when I heard the knock at the door. "Shoot." I quickly turned off the taps, stepped out and grabbed a towel. In my haste to get myself together and then answer the door, the dodgy floorboard didn't even register until my foot slammed through it, snagging my ankle and bringing me to my knees.

I yelled as I fell, and cursed. Wincing, I looked at my predicament, trying to yank my foot out as I did so. A loud groan slipped past my lips. This was no good. I was wedged, and it appeared I'd lost my towel in my fall. *Just great.*

CHAPTER FOUR

TANNER

I LOOKED ONCE MORE AT THE PAPERWORK, MAKING sure I had the right address. 52 Ledgebrook Avenue. Glancing at the tilted, rusty plaque on the house, I saw the number matched up. I raised my brows... even the plaque needed replacing.

When I'd been called in to give a quote for a refurb, the guy had told me the place needed a lot of work, but from what I could see from the outside, it needed gutting. Not that I couldn't do with the work, but it wasn't what I'd been expecting.

I folded my paperwork and tucked it in the back pocket of my jeans before switching my phone to silent and rapping my knuckles on the paint-peeled door. As I waited, my gaze roamed to the windows, wooden and old, a few cracked panes. The place was easily a hundred years old and didn't look like it had received much looking after over the years. It was a building that with time and love, and a crapload of cash, could easily be beautiful again.

A thump followed by a bang and a curse drew my eyes back to the closed door. I grinned and lifted my brow, wondering whether it was the house's dilapidated state that had caused the groaned curse.

I'd never been to this part of town before. Never had a reason to. Lined with old oaks, all the properties set well back from the street, it seemed like a nice place, even more so, I imagined, in its heyday. It bugged the crap out of me when places like this went to wreck and ruin, but without it, I'd be outta work, so I was in no position to complain.

Another thirty seconds passed, and the door remained closed, and the sound of cursing had stopped. Lifting my hand up once more, I knocked again. "Hello?" Who knew what had happened to the guy. The thud had been heavy, and the curse expelled with a masculine groan. "You good—" I tugged the paperwork back out of my pocket and searched for the name. "—Carter? Everything all right in there?"

The sound of shuffling and a low moan reached my ears. *Damn.* I grabbed the handle, turned and pushed. The door creaked open. Knocking as I pushed it open further, I called out, "Hey, it's Tanner. I'm here to give you a quote. You okay?"

"Oh heck." The light curse was much louder as I stood in the hallway, and it came from upstairs. "Yeah." The voice was an equal mix of pained and pissed off. "Up here."

I looked toward the staircase, my brow furrowing when I took in the state of the banister, or what was left of it. After closing the door behind me, I made my way to the bottom of the staircase. "You need some help?" I called, eyes roaming the joint.

It was clear from the scattering of boxes and the used wine glass placed on a small table next to the sofa in the sitting room that the place was lived in, but fuck, the house was a wreck.

From ceiling to floor, to doors, to some wood paneling, the joint needed a serious overhaul.

A voice cleared with a light cough. "Er, crap, yeah, I think so. I'm kinda stuck."

Rather than racing up the stairs and risk my foot smashing through a rotten board, I made my way up carefully, staying close to the wall. The stairs had a landing halfway up and then angled to the right. Once there, my eyes were immediately drawn to a guy on the floor, butt naked.

My eyes widened when they landed on his form. Damn, it wasn't every day a client greeted me in the nude. Looking at the path between me and who I assumed to be Carter on the ground, I tried not to let my eyes linger for too long on his smooth expanse of skin. He was lightly toned, with a softness about him that was impossible to not notice, despite trying my hardest not to.

With a shake of my head, I calculated each step I took to get to his side. Once I made it safely to the top, the floorboards creaking under my booted feet, Carter angled himself to turn and look at me. Definitely pissed off and in pain, and perhaps a bit mortified too, a light blush covering his cheeks. His gaze roamed me from bottom to top before landing on my own. I quirked my brow in amusement and question while strategically ignoring how fucking pretty his brown eyes were. "So...?" I offered.

He sighed, and I watched in fascination as his Adam's apple bobbed when he swallowed. "I rushed from the piece-of-crap shower when I heard the knock. My foot went through the board, and it's stuck." His pink cheeks turned crimson.

Unable to stay the small smile tugging at my lips, I grinned as I stepped closer. I took my time to get to him, wanting to help the guy out. The last thing he needed was me falling on my ass. Clearing my throat, I crouched down at his side, my focus now on his leg and foot.

The whole area was rotten and would need ripping out. But for the time being, I'd need to tear up the two surrounding boards to get his ankle free. "You have tried to get it out, right?" I felt like a jackass for asking, but it was always best to check first.

Carter huffed out a breath. "Yeah, I did. It's wedged against something. I tried pulling it out, but it's a no go. It's tighter than a virgin ass."

My gaze whipped to his. *What the fuck?* With lifted brows, I stared wide-eyed at him, drawing another blush from him.

"Shoot, sorry. That was inappropriate." His eyes widened in horror. "I meant, it's wedged. Erm. It's just wedged tight, and—"

I grinned. "It's all good. Give me a sec." The poor guy looked like he wanted to join his foot in the space under the floorboards and curl over. He needed an out, and I needed to get some air in my lungs away from his intoxicating smell and firm thighs, which were impossible to ignore in such close proximity.

The guy was attractive. I'd taken note immediately but pushed the knowledge aside. Work and eyeing up hot guys or potential clients was never a smart move.

I stood and headed down the stairs, throwing over my shoulder, "Let me just get a couple of tools."

"Okay. Thanks." His voice was low, awkwardness still evident. I wondered if he was trying to recover from his ass reference, and couldn't help but wonder if it'd been intentional, to test the waters, or Christ, perhaps it was just his sense of humor. Either way, my interest was piqued.

WITH THE FRESH AIR CAME CLARITY. THERE WAS NO way I could risk a job of this size and this potential cash for the sake of getting blown. As much as his dark brown eyes had captured my attention and stirred me to life, there were other places I could visit to get an itch scratched if I was that desperate. Admittedly, it would be a lengthy drive to get there, but Davis's words were still in my mind from the previous night.

Refocused and determined not to react to the insanely sexy cut of Carter's jaw, I kneeled by his foot —after throwing him a towel to cover his groin, which I may have given a lingering glance—and began the task of freeing his foot. In less than five minutes, I had him released. His ankle was swollen and grazed, but declaring himself a veterinarian—whatever that had to do with human bones I had no clue—Carter was sure it was just bruised and sprained.

I helped him up, acutely aware that I held my breath when I clasped him close to steady him. He was virtually the same height as me, just shy a couple of inches from my six two. The perfect height for any angle. Mentally smacking myself around my head, I dragged my overeager thoughts out of the gutter and helped him to his room.

"Thanks, Tanner. I'm good. I should be all right to sort myself out and get down the stairs."

I nodded but wasn't convinced as I hovered in the open doorway. It had nothing to do with him being perched on the bed wrapped in a small towel, most of his body on display. I closed my eyes for the briefest of seconds, giving myself time to sort my crap out. Once opened, his eyes were on my chest before landing on my face and connecting with mine. I cleared my throat. "Sure. Do you want me to have a quick look around the place while you're dressing? I'll make some notes from what I can see, and then downstairs you can talk me through anything else."

He smiled, and I wished he hadn't. I'd had plenty of quick fucks in my time, and a couple of serious relationships, but Carter was something else. Clean-cut, and so not my usual type, as I tended to go for rough and rugged, but when he smiled my gut lurched and my dick sprung to life.

"That would be great, thanks. I'm sure I'd hold you up hobbling. And don't get me wrong, I can see you're sporting some guns there, but I wouldn't have thought you'd want to be carrying me around." His grin widened, and he laughed. It was surprisingly deep and absolutely genuine.

"Right." Like a deer in headlights, I froze a moment then pussied on out of there, not taking the bait. If that was what it was. Fuck, I was so confused by everything that had happened in the last twenty minutes or so. "Err, just shout if you need me." I pulled the door closed behind me, or at least attempted to. It wouldn't latch shut.

It was going to be a long list and a painful meeting. My thoughts were too focused on picking Carter up and holding him close as I bucked into him. The possibility drifted to the forefront of my mind. *Fuck. I'm screwed.*

disliking feeling out of my depth. "So, the house, when you said it needed a lot of work, you weren't kidding."

He sighed. "Yes, I know." Taking a gulp of his drink, he glanced around the space before looking back at me. "It needs doing. There's no getting out of it."

I nodded before handing him my notes, giving him a few moments to look over them. "There's also the attic that needs work. The insulation has sagged and ripped in parts. The roof looks fine, but what do I know?" he added with a laugh. "The hatch has one of those pull-down ladders if you want to pop your head up? The opening is in the back bedroom."

I stood, giving him a smile. "I'll take a look now." Once up the stairs, I found the opening, pulled down the steps and poked my head up. Removing the small flashlight from my belt, I looked around the open space. The roof did look fine, plus there was no damp from what I could see. But all the insulation would need tearing down and replacing. The poor guy would need a lot of dough to be able to fit out this place to spec. Shaking my head, I made my way downstairs, hoping he wouldn't be too horrified when he received my quote.

His eyes were on me as soon as I entered the

kitchen. "Uh-oh! By that grim expression, I'm assuming it's not a simple patch-up?"

I offered him a light smile. "Sorry, man. It's not actually a hard job, just messy and expensive to replace the whole insulation for the area."

"Figures," he mumbled.

I stood awkwardly at the door, wishing there was something I could do to help him out. He seemed like a nice guy, obviously as hot as sin, and it was clear he hadn't signed up for this mammoth task. "Have you thought about just selling it?" I offered.

With a small shrug, he answered, "I did have that passing thought, especially when I first came, but not so much anymore."

I nodded in understanding. "I can get a quote to you in a few days. There are just some materials I need to price up first." I cleared my throat uncomfortably. "You know the materials alone are going to cost you, right?" I tried to keep my face blank but was sure my regret was transparent.

A smile lit up his face, and I grinned back, finding it impossible not to. "It's all good. Just give me a fair quote, and we'll be good."

"Okay, well, I best be going." I hesitated. "Thanks for the coffee." He made to stand. "Please, I can find my way out. Just keep off your ankle." I grimaced internally as the desire to protect him surged through me. I needed to get on the road before I offered to piggyback him where he needed to go, or something as equally stupid.

"Thanks." He grinned. "We'll chat soon, yeah?"

I nodded dumbly, wanting nothing more than to chat about the prospect of a date, but knowing it was completely inappropriate. He threw me a weak smile just before I turned and left, my heart beating ridiculously fast while my dick remained unwilling to play hard to get. "Yeah, see ya," I called over my shoulder as I hightailed it out of there.

CHAPTER FIVE

TANNER

FOR THREE DAYS, I'D BEEN BARTERING PRICES FROM local merchants to get Carter the best price going. I'd finally pulled enough favors to get him a good deal. Even though the quote seemed crazy high and would have most men balking at the cost, I knew it was low. My prices alone for labor would be barely enough to keep me afloat, but my property out East was finally under contract, plus, what was a man to do when his dick was leading him?

After finalizing the quote, it would be an easy task to e-mail it to him. It seemed, though, I was a glutton for punishment. Instead, I pulled up to his house. It was past seven o'clock in the evening, but like a needy fucker, I wanted to make sure I could hand it to him personally rather than leaving it in his mailbox.

I looked down at my grubby work clothes, and reached for the spare shirt I kept in my truck. I tugged on the clean T-shirt then pulled out my body spray and doused myself, not wanting to offend the guy, and then grabbed his quote. I hesitated at his door, remembering our first and last encounter. It wasn't every day I had the chance to see a fine cock on display within the first five seconds of meeting someone. I'd got an eyeful though with Carter, certainly a good enough view that it had fed my imagination the last few days.

Sighing deeply to calm my increased heart rate, I composed myself enough to knock on the door. This time there were no screams or cries for help. Instead, I heard soft padding feet make their way to the door before it opened. A barefooted Carter stood before me, wearing jeans and a chest-hugging tee. He looked every bit as sexy as I remembered.

"Hey, Tanner." A bright smile lit up his face. "Come in." He backed away from the door and headed to the kitchen. I noticed he was no longer limping, which was good. "Close it behind you, please. I have food on the stove."

I swallowed as I watched him walk away, my gaze

me to do anything?" I asked, feeling like an idiot as I stood staring at him.

Still stirring the pot he held in his hand, he nodded and indicated the fridge. "There's beer and white wine in the fridge. Red's just on the counter. Help yourself." He then turned and set about finishing the food.

Exhaling, I cracked my neck, trying to relieve some of the tension that sat on my shoulders. "Beer's good, thanks. What are you having?"

"Red, please. The glasses are just to the right of my head."

After shooting off a quick text to Davis letting him know I wouldn't be over to help with Libby at bath time, I held back the groan when he immediately texted me back offering me his words of wisdom.

Davis: Behave and if you can't keep it in your pants, make sure you give the best head ever. Stop being a fucking pussy!

It may not have been my smartest move to tell him about Carter and how fucking hot he was. Davis hadn't let up since then. He'd been actively encouraging me to screw my no-fraternizing rule, which he'd said was "the biggest pile-of-crap excuse" he'd ever heard. I knew he was onto something, but there was no way I'd tell him that.

After turning my phone to silent and shoving it in my pocket, I ventured over to where Carter stood, stepped around him, and reached up, my chest brushing against his back. I swallowed hard when his intake of breath hit my ears. *Retreat, retreat,* sounded in my head, even though it was the last thing my cock wanted. Clenching my jaw as I stopped myself from reaching out and doing something stupid, I quickly swiped a glass from the shelf, grabbed the bottle of wine, and headed straight for the fridge. The distance helped—a little.

After I'd sorted our drinks, I went to the table and sat down, watching Carter flitter around the kitchen, organizing the dinnerware, straining the pasta, and then finally dishing up. I took the opportunity to get myself under control and put my game face on. Mixing business with pleasure was never a good idea. While it could be all sorts of fun, Carter's job would take months to complete. If it had been a quick one, I was sure I would have already pounced on him by the time he'd put the plate in front of me. But it wasn't. Any sort of play would have been an asshole move. Relationships could so quickly get screwed, which would make what I can do is stop by a few days a week to begin the demo." His smile was back, along with his brows lifted in surprise.

"I can't expect you to—"

"Honestly, I want to. It's all good. I can make a good start while materials are on order. It will mean you'll need to limit room usage. I'll start in the attic and work my way down. Eventually, you'll be living out of three rooms. One of the bathrooms, your bedroom, and the kitchen. But we'll figure it all out." I wasn't quite sure how we'd figure it out, but we'd cross that bridge when we came to it in a few months.

"Well, three days a week, I finish work early at two, so maybe those days I could help you out? That way I can be here to move things out of your way." He laughed. "I could be your laborer."

I raised my brow at his suggestion. Never, in all my years in the trade, had I ever allowed a client to assist. Clients could be pains in the ass and often got in the way. Not only that, but they were potentially a huge insurance headache waiting to happen.

Carter took a gulp of his wine, looking especially pleased with himself. "I have a tool belt and tools I've been wanting to break in." He paused, his gaze landing on mine. "Erm, if that's okay. I promise not to get under your feet. I'll be where you need me to be and do exactly what you tell me to." He gave a one-shoulder shrug and offered me a small smile.

I inwardly groaned. With an offer like that, there was no way I could refuse. Plus his enthusiasm was sexy as fuck. I cleared my throat before speaking, pushing the thought of Carter bending to my will aside. "Sure. I could do with your help. More hands, less work and all that." I paused. "But no power tools and no falling through any floorboards."

He raised his glass toward me and I clinked my bottle against it. "Cheers, Tanner. I think this is all going to be perfect."

I smiled and hoped I wouldn't regret bending the rules.

CHAPTER SIX

CARTER

THE LAST THREE WEEKS HAD BEEN TORTURE, AND IT seemed I was an eager fool. Every minute I wasn't with Tanner, I spent thinking about him. The thoughts left me desperate and needy. If that wasn't bad enough, I'd had hard-ons at the most awkward of times when I should have been focusing on an animal's balls rather than my own.

On top of that, the three nights a week and Saturdays that I'd managed to get time with him left me so frustrated, I was sure I would die from blue balls. All I'd discovered about Tanner made me lust after him even more. He was patient to a T, putting up with my incessant questions and my getting in the way. We'd quickly discovered that I was ridiculously clumsy. I was convinced this was to do with my blood rushing to all manner of areas when I was around him, considering I usually had a steady hand and nerves—pretty much needed when operating on an animal. It seemed that I also wasn't much use at ripping stuff out. It was crazy. How hard was it to tear down a ceiling or a wall? Apparently, not so easy, well, not for me anyway. The last time I tried, I ended up tearing through some wiring.

So, after a few rounds of realizing my help could be more of a hindrance, I was tasked with cleanup and garbage removal duty, which my aching muscles could attest to. Plus, I was chief coffee maker and chef. Admittedly, I had every intention of ensuring I fed Tanner a good meal at the end of every evening he came by. I'd expected more of a fight from him when I insisted on cooking for him, sure he'd have to rush off home, but after our first after-work meal of steak and trimmings, he'd readily agreed.

Those meals had become the best parts of my week. While I loved watching him work and get all sweaty and dirty, it was the ease of our conversation over food that kept me going, and of course tortured me.

"Are you about wrapped up? Dinner will be in fifteen." I stood at the bottom of the ladder looking up at Tanner and not so discreetly staring at his perfect butt. His jeans molded his ass, leaving little to my overactive imagination. The fact that it was framed with a tool belt made him even more levels of hot.

My gaze lifted to his face when he spoke and angled to look at me. His raised brow indicated he'd seen me checking him out. I clamped my jaw shut, willing my embarrassment to not travel to my cheeks. "Sure. I'm all done," he said. "I just need to move the boards to the dumpster."

"I can do that." I smiled and then looked at the stack of broken boards to my right.

"They're pretty heavy. We can do them together." I nodded and watched as he climbed down the ladder, my hands on the sides keeping it steady for him. His feet touched the ground while I remained in position, his back a mere inch from my chest.

Flip! His closeness, his scent, both washed over me. I released a shaky breath and realized I needed to release the ladder and take a step back. Instead, I remained frozen until Tanner cleared his throat. I let go of the ladder and backed up, banging into materials piled behind me. In slow motion, I flailed, my eyes on Tanner as he turned. His eyes widened in horror.

I was tumbling and knew there was no soft landing around me. A moment before I hit the ground, strong hands grabbed me, one on the front of my shirt, the other on my arm. I jerked to a stop as Tanner tugged, helping me find my balance. In the process, buttons flew and material tore as my shirt was ripped open. I clasped his arms as I steadied myself, my heart pounding erratically.

"You okay?" Tanner was out of breath, still wide-eyed and closer than I'd realized.

I raised my head to look better into his eyes and nodded. "Yes." My voice was barely a whisper as I willed my heart to calm, an impossible task considering I was in the arms of the man I'd been dreaming of since the day I met him. "Thank you."

A smile lifted his mouth, finally washing away the panic from his eyes. He released my arm, his hand moving to my face as he swept at my cheek. I stopped breathing. Honest to God, forgot to inhale and take air into my lungs at the contact. The moment was over all too quickly. His eyes flashed with an emotion I couldn't quite figure out before he stepped away from me. "Umm, you had dust on your cheek." He then cleared his throat, his eyes landing on my chest. "Erm, sorry about that." A slow color crept up his neck, dusting his jaw and cheeks.

was enough to have nervous excitement bubbling in my chest.

"Actually, I'll start on Friday. The day of the delivery. Everything else should be wrapped up by then, so I should be set."

Grinning, I placed down my glass. "Perfect." I bit my bottom lip while I built the courage to pry a bit further. "So I imagine you can have your Saturdays back." I smiled, though it was a little forced. "I imagine the…" I faltered. *Screw it.* "…man in your life will be happy with that." I kept my smile fixed in place and watched him carefully. There were so many potential scenarios for the outcome. The worst being a punch to the jaw and him walking off the job for suggesting he was gay.

He stopped eating, putting his cutlery down before bringing his beer to his lips. His eyes remained on me the whole time. It was torture, and by the glint in his eye, the sexy bastard knew it. He placed his bottle down, rested his elbows on the table, and leaned forward slightly. He angled his head to the side. "I'll be here on Saturday." He grinned, leaned back, picked up his fork and shoveled lasagna into his mouth.

What did that even mean? Frowning, I squinted at him. I wasn't great at looking hardass. That was confirmed when he laughed and took another swig of beer. I lifted a brow at him in challenge. I needed him to answer the stinkin' question already, but he seemed far too amused by my wayward attempt at prying information out of him.

"You okay?" he asked, amusement dancing in his eyes.

"Fine." The word came out as a sigh.

Leaning forward again, Tanner asked, "You have something you want to ask me?"

He was really going to make me ask. Why did it feel like I was in high school again? Not that my high school experience was anything like this, at all actually. Absorbing the amusement rolling off him, I smiled. How could I not when such a fine specimen of man was playing me?

"Do you date men?"

I said it. Despite feeling slightly moronic, relief filtered through me. I *really* needed to know. Did I have a chance or not?

He pursed his lips into a small smile that made it seem like he held back laughter. With his hands cupped before him, elbows on the table, he brushed a thumb across his bottom lip. I followed every movement, wishing more than anything to replace his thumb with my tongue.

"Yes. I date men." I wasn't sure if his voice had dipped low or I was simply hoping it had. "I'm not dating right now. There's no man, boyfriend, lover, or husband waiting for me at home." He paused a moment before he continued, "I do have a brother, well, my friend, and a niece who I spend a lot of time with, and I help them out whenever I can. He's a new dad and a single parent." I nodded in understanding. Heck, Tanner was such a good guy, and his commitment to his family upped his sexiness from hot to scorching. "Davis is doing better though and is actively kicking my ass to get out from under his feet." He grinned, seemingly amused by his brother. "I'll put in a few Saturdays to get ahead of the work, too. If that's okay?" With his hands still in the same position before him, his thumb resting on his bottom lip, his eyes focused on mine.

"Yes." I practically squeaked the word. My heart pounded hard in my chest while my tightening pants were making it impossibly difficult to concentrate on anything else. It was in celebratory mode, currently sitting up and taking complete notice of Tanner's mouth and thumb. I cleared my throat. "Saturdays are perfect. You're more than welcome here whenever you need." I grinned.

Nodding, he nibbled on the end of his thumb.

While he still held the same confidence as earlier, his teasing seemed to have vanished. This time when he spoke, his voice was definitely deeper. "So with my new key I can come by whenever and not worry about interrupting you or anything?"

I shook my head immediately. What little cool I had went flying out the window and into the gutter with my dirty thoughts. "I'm not dating anyone. It's been a while. While this place is friendly enough, it's not the easiest place to meet a guy, you know?" Embarrassment flushed through me. What if he thought I was only interested because there were slim pickings? Hell, that couldn't be further from the truth. In the short amount of time I'd known Tanner, everything I'd discovered, I liked. A lot. "Shoot, erm…." Heat rushed over me, but I was too far gone to hold back. "I don't want you to think I'm hitting on you just because you're gay."

I considered jumping up and down in hopes that the floor would swallow me whole. My brain cells had vanished along with my ability to not sound like a turd.

"I mean…." What the hell did I mean?

Both of Tanner's brows were high as he watched me struggle to extract my foot out of my mouth. "What? What did you mean?" he asked.

I clamped my mouth closed before blowing out a breath of air, puffing out my cheeks. I shrugged. A loud laugh burst from Tanner, and I grinned in relief.

"So you're not hitting on me then? Is that it?"

My grin slipped. How on earth was I to answer that? While his smile remained in place, the air between us became charged. I opened my mouth to speak, but before I could, he said, "I'm joking." But there was no humor in his eyes. "It's all good. I'm pleased we cleared the air." He looked at his watch. "But I need to get going. It's getting late, so we best get all this cleared up." Standing, he picked up both of our plates and headed to the sink, leaving me sitting dumbstruck.

I had no idea what had happened. The tension had been there, and not in the "I'm going to knock you out" kind of way. I was sure he'd felt something for me too. Could I have misread him completely?

I SAID GOODBYE TO TANNER AT THE DOOR BEFORE handing him the spare key. With a "thanks," he'd left, not once looking behind him. Sighing, I finished tidying up and made my way to my room. I had an earlier start the next day than usual with a staff meeting, so I needed an early night. But sleep didn't come swiftly. Instead, I lay awake for far too long thinking about Tanner.

He confused the sense out of me. I wasn't an idiot to think just because he'd winked a few times he'd be interested. Christ, that would be a dick move of mine. I flirted with guys and women all the time, and usually—obviously when it came to flirting with women—it was nothing to do with attraction. It meant jack shit. I was a flirt and always had been; it came as naturally to me as breathing. So Tanner baffled me. His unobtrusive flirting moments, his friendly nature, there were times when I convinced myself real attraction fed those. But over dinner I received the message loud and clear. He wasn't interested.

I was no novice and had been in a couple of fairly serious relationships since school, but nothing had ever stuck. I was far from desperate to settle down. Hell, I was only twenty-nine, but I saw something in Tanner that was different. And the crux was, that indescribable feeling, the invisible connection pulsing inside me, whether he was near or far, had my heart sitting up and paying attention. He made me want more, imagine something bigger, something real and palpable. And once I worked out what exactly it was, I didn't know if I'd be able to let it go.

The thought terrified me after his brush-off at dinner. For an intelligent man, I'd been sidestepping labeling my feelings and acting dumb. I thought that was the safe play. It seemed I was wrong, because frick me, I was falling for Tanner hard and fast.

With Tanner on my mind and the memory of his hands on my arm when he'd stopped me from falling on my ass, I eventually drifted into sleep, not sure whether my dreaming of him was the healthiest thing for me to do.

MY ALARM BLARED AT STUPID O'CLOCK. GRUMBLING, I shut it off and prepared for work. Just thirty minutes later, I was heading out to the clinic, hoping that Denver, the director of Holmes Veterinary Clinic, wouldn't spend too long droning on. He was a nice enough boss but had a habit of not knowing when to shut up and let us get on with it. The guy's heart was in the right place, so it was hard to be too frustrated at him. It didn't make the journey into work just as the sun was rising any easier though.

After parking, I made my way inside. Lauren greeted me with a grin and a takeout coffee. "For me?" I threw her a thankful grin. "You know I'm yours and will worship you forever, right?"

Lauren laughed and rolled her eyes. "Yes, I have a tab going, and one day I will call it in." She handed me the cup.

I kissed her on the cheek. "Thank you so much, Lauren." I inhaled the fresh scent and then brought it to my lips. The magical coffee hit my tongue, and my brain gave a little cheer, promising to start functioning soon. "You are an angel. Seriously." She really was.

I'd liked Lauren instantly. Not only was she a caffeine addict like me, but she also had divine taste in men. I could happily talk movies and models with her.

"So have you heard the latest?" Her voice took on the tone of conspirator, and she angled her face toward me.

I quirked my brow and grinned. Lowering my own voice, I asked, "I'm assuming not. What gives?"

"Well, Denver's taking a three-month sabbatical." She paused to take in my reaction. My eyebrows rising to my hairline was apparently the correct response, as she smirked before continuing. "He's announcing his temporary replacement today." How this woman managed to get the intel was beyond me, but she always seemed to be one step ahead.

"Any idea who?" I had no grand dream of being announced. Not only was I new to the clinic, but I was also the youngest by far. I imagined Terry would step up. He was in his fifties and would do a good job at managing the place. I paused at the thought. Something didn't add up. "Why are you all cloak and dagger about this?" It wasn't a big deal for Terry or even Holly to take on the position.

Lauren chewed on her bottom lip, barely containing her excitement. If that tell wasn't a dead giveaway, her gripping my forearm was. "He's brought someone in from the outside."

"Oh." I was genuinely surprised.

"Apparently, he's Denver's nephew or cousin's nephew, or erm, I'm not sure." A faraway, dreamy look cast over her features. "Just you wait." She sighed elaborately, her breath causing her bangs to lift and sway.

So the dude was a hottie. Interesting. I always appreciated a bit of sex god in my day. Intrigued, we edged closer to the meeting room door and entered just as Denver cleared his throat to begin. We quickly took our seats, and I glanced around the room. All the familiar faces were present. There was no mystery nephew or whatever relation.

Sitting back, I half listened to Denver talking about a new product coming in, before he droned on about a pharmacy rep visiting the following week. It took everything in me not to drift off completely, but I remained semi-alert. As soon as he mentioned sabbatical, my ears perked up, and I raised my gaze to look at him. It seemed Scott Anderson, his godson, was due to arrive to hold down the fort. Denver reeled off an impressive list of qualifications and positions, so much so it was obvious why Scott would be taking over.

"I know all this seems very sudden, but sometimes when an opportunity presents itself, it can't be ignored," Denver said immediately after telling us he'd be leaving in a week. "That's all the time Scott will need to get a feel for the place," he praised.

He had high hopes for sure. While we weren't a huge practice, we were growing, and popular. Plus we had a large collection of some smaller communities. It was easy to come in as a vet. We could just roll up our sleeves and get the job done, but learning the systems and running of the place I'd assumed took a little more than that. Either I was dead wrong, or this Scott truly was a veterinary god.

I paused at that thought and looked at Lauren. She flicked her gaze to me in question. "How do you know this guy's a hottie?" I asked in a hushed voice.

She grinned with mischief. "I grabbed his name off Denver's desk and stalked him on Facebook," she whispered.

I gave a low snort. This woman was a serious menace but very handy to have around. I watched as she pulled her phone from her pocket. She placed it low under the table and clicked away before nudging me. I surreptitiously leaned closer to her, eyes focusing on the image.

A smiling man stared back from the picture with a chiseled jaw and gorgeous gray eyes. I understood Lauren's reaction. He was handsome all right, in a clean-cut sleek sort of way. Traditionally handsome, Scott had it covered. He was no Tanner though. The comparison made me pause. Tanner was a little unkempt, with a hot bod, and a smile that made my heart flip ridiculously. Scott definitely didn't get that reaction. There was also something missing in the eyes of the man in the photo. While pretty to look at, the smile on his lips didn't meet them. It was curious, really. A man who looked like that, with a resume like his, goodness, what did he have to be unhappy about?

Lauren switched off her phone, wrapping her hands around the device. Making eye contact with her, I barely held back my chuckle as she waggled her brows up and down like a crazy woman. "Right?" she asked.

I gave a noncommittal shrug, a small smile playing on my lips. "Done better."

Her loud snort drew the attention of the room.

"You okay there, Lauren?" Denver asked.

Nodding quickly, she dragged her lips between her teeth, reining in her need to break into laughter. I did the same.

IT WAS ALMOST TWO O'CLOCK WHEN DENVER STEPPED into my examining room. I'd had pretty much back-to-back clients all day. Everything routine, which was nice after the hellish case I'd had the previous week involving a rabbit and a key. I looked up when he entered, his godson in tow.

"Carter, Scott Anderson," Denver introduced. The same smile from his photo was fixed in place. Before Denver could continue with introductions, his name was called from along the corridor. "Excuse me a minute. You two carry on." Denver smiled before leaving us alone.

"Good to meet you," I greeted. I smiled and stepped forward, stretching out my hand. Scott took it, giving a firm shake before taking a small step back. "Your journey okay?"

He nodded, glancing around the room before his gaze almost reluctantly settled on mine. "Yes, thank you. It was a trek, but I'm here now."

"That you are," I answered, feeling the need to fill in the pregnant pause. I hated awkwardness and silence. I handled neither well, always ending up blabbering on about irrelevant nonsense when the situation arose. "So, where are you staying?"

His jaw twitched before he answered a little too casually, "Oh, I'll be taking over Denver's place. He's heading off on his travels and such."

Again with the awkward silence. "Oh great. That's just a few doors down from my place. We'll be neighbors." From the blanch on his face, it was clear I was being too peppy. I attempted to tone it down. "So if you need anything, just holler."

He gave a brief nod before glancing at the door.

"I'm sure Denver's waiting to introduce you to everyone." I offered him an escape, which he took with barely a goodbye. The door closing behind him, I stood there a little dumbstruck. What the hell was that all about? The guy was bizarrely on edge and pretty much weird. Shrugging it off, I finished clearing up my equipment and tidying the room, ready to head home. My workday had officially ended on a weird note, and I couldn't wait to get home to see Tanner.

I sighed at the thought—home and Tanner—not liking how I was counting the one as being synonymous with the other. After last night's frustrating conversation, it was clear that Tanner wasn't interested. While I wasn't fine with that—okay, I was so disappointed my heart hurt—it was probably for the best. As much as I wanted him, I'd hate for something to go wrong that could screw up his working on the house, but more importantly, I'd hate to miss out on his company.

Our dinners, our conversations, my annoying him while trying to be helpful—I looked forward to those times. They'd filled up so many lonely hours. He made my day brighter and made my heart that much lighter. It wasn't something I was willing to give up. Attraction be damned.

I waved goodbye to the staff, making sure I found Lauren before leaving. She was busy, so I didn't have time to chat with her about Scott Analson. Admittedly, I wasn't great with nicknames, but I amused myself and smiled at the thought. Telling her we'd catch up the next day, I made my way to my car and headed home.

The journey was quick and uneventful, exactly how I liked my journeys. I wasn't quite sure how I'd cope in the city if I ever decided to return. The quietness of the town was a mix of a blessing and a curse. I loved how laid-back it was, the slower pace, but I hadn't realized how isolating the quiet could be. I'd been out a few times with Lauren since relocating, but she regularly had hookups, so I'd put off going out for the evening. No one liked being the man sitting by himself in a bar, especially not the gay man in the bar.

I'd had a few mishaps in the town, unsurprising considering the nature of the small-town mentality, but disappointing nonetheless. Fortunately, there were also good people around, especially helpful that several were hardass farmers who I'd gained the respect of since working with them and their cattle. But still, drunk bigots whispering "faggot" none too quietly had a way of ruining and cutting short a night.

I pulled up at my house, smiling at Tanner's truck parked in the driveway. A wave of calm flowed over me knowing he was already at my house and hard at work. It would be easy to be swept away by that feeling if I allowed it to control me, but I couldn't. I could do friendship with Tanner, even if it made me miserable. I snorted at the thought. Because however miserable my heart was, it was battling it out with the happiness camping there.

CHAPTER SEVEN

TANNER

Hey, honey, you're home! The temptation was on the tip of my tongue when I heard the front door open and then close, but I held it back. It had been a month since our "gay" conversation, and the tension had only recently dissipated completely. Finally, our easygoing exchanges were back on form, and we'd reached the place where banter was comfortable and friendly flirting was natural if not a little dangerous.

I'd tried not to flirt with Carter, but that was as difficult as not breathing and inhaling his scent when he brushed past me. I liked spending time with him, and winding down over dinner was the highlight of my day. The last few nights I'd hung around after dinner too. One night we'd made a halfhearted attempt at watching a movie. Just thirty minutes in and we were chatting about everything from childhood memories to whether humans would one day live on Mars. It had been midnight before I'd left. Crazy since I'd returned six hours later to start work, but that was just how it was.

There was no doubt that I spent most of my time at his house. While I worked a lot of hours, more than I probably would have on another job, I also spent most of my free time with Carter too. The little voice inside my head would chant "Danger" to me every now and then, but every time I brushed it aside. I was in control. Or at least that was what I told said voice.

Initially I'd felt guilty as hell about Davis and Libby. I'd gone from spending virtually all my free time with the two of them to dropping by every other day, sometimes just three times a week. I still spoke to or texted Davis every day, but the guilt rode me hard.

About three weeks or so earlier Davis had sat me down with a beer and a stern expression. I'd been freaked out initially as it was clear something serious had been on his mind. Apparently the serious talk was an intervention of sorts. At first, I'd laughed it off and lovingly told him to fuck off—until I'd realized how serious he was.

"Tanner, fuck, man. I love you like a brother, and I'll never be able to repay you for everything you've done for Libby and me. Damn, you saved us both."

I scoffed. He was being ridiculously OTT.

Davis shook his head. "Don't, I'm serious. When you stepped in, and hell... moved your whole life to support me —" He swallowed hard, emotion swirling in his eyes. I shifted uncomfortably. He was my brother in every way but blood, but fuck, I hated getting emotional. "—you showed me I could do this. I couldn't manage, be a dad. I was a fucking mess and had no one."

I made to interrupt, but he shook his head.

"I know I had you, but damn, the thought of asking you for help... yet you were there for me, still are. I love you, man. Seriously. But fuck, I need you to go and get a fucking life."

His grin contrasted with the seriousness of his words. Laughter burst from my chest, leaving me coughing with how quickly it had ripped from me.

"Seriously? You're telling me to fuck off and get out of your hair?"

He nodded, his grin wide, eyes serious, and not a shadow of uncertainty or jest evident. "Yeah. Don't get me wrong, I still want you to be here. Fuck, just the thought of Libby growing up and having to handle all the jerks *who'll be after her by myself is making me get gray fucking hairs already. I'll need you for that.*

"It's just... it seems like life's settling down for you. Work's going well, then there's Carter." *He waggled his brows, and I shook my head.*

"What's Carter have to do with anything?" *Davis hadn't even met him, but then why would he have? Carter's a client, I reminded myself.*

Davis rolled his eyes so dramatically I thought he'd give himself an injury. "I can't believe you're still fooling yourself. I've never seen you this hung up on a guy and you haven't even kissed the dude." *He paused.* "Hold on, have you had some and not told me, you dirty fucker?"

"No." *I laughed, shaking my head.* "Nothing's happened."

"But you want it to happen." *His response was 100 percent statement and 110 percent accurate.*

I sighed. "Heck yeah. He's so fucking hot, and sexy, and he's so goddamn smart and sweet and witty." *I stopped when Davis's expression turned almost comical. His eyebrows popped up so high they virtually touched his hairline. It was teamed with a goofy grin.* "What?" *I sighed.*

"I'm picturing little love hearts forming in your eyes. It's... strangely cute and... totally fucking weird." *His laughter then died down.* "Just get over whatever shit's *holding you back and preventing you from seeing where this thing with Carter may lead, and don't worry about Libby and me. She knows her uncle Tanner loves her and will break bones for her, but get a life."* It was my turn for my eyebrows to shoot up. *"I'm serious. I* need *you to have a life, find your own happiness."*

I closed my eyes, not quite sure how to process everything he'd said to me. I knew, deep in my gut, every word he spoke was true; it didn't stop me worrying about him though.

"Hey," I called down, letting Carter know the general direction I was in.

A murmured "Hey" was almost indiscernible. I paused. Something was wrong for sure. Every single day without fail, Carter would stride my way, a sexy-as-fuck smile on his face, greeting me like I'd just solved world peace or something. Each and every time, I'd always have to calm my breathing and prevent the hitch escaping when I drank him in after not seeing him for the day. It was bad. Fuck, I *had* it bad.

I placed down my saw and propped the plank against the wall. The pull to check on him was strong. There was no way to ignore it. I found him in the kitchen, a glass of wine in his hand and him topping it up. While leaning against the doorframe, I watched him gulp down the whole glass before he placed both the bottle and the glass on the worktop. He placed his hands flat down on the surface and lowered his head.

I'd never seen him like this. Ever. While I'd not known Carter all that long, after the hours we'd spent together, I was sure I knew him better than most of my friends, with the exception of Davis, and more than any boyfriend I'd had. I didn't spare a thought to that, not quite sure what that said about me and my past relationships. But Carter, I knew him.

"Hey," I greeted again, my voice low in an attempt to soothe and not startle. "You want to talk about it?"

He shook his head, not turning to look at me.

He was hurting, that much was obvious. There was only one other way I could think of to deal with it, short of offering him a blow job, which I'd foolishly promised myself I wouldn't do. "Want something harder?" I clamped my mouth shut. I wasn't quite sure if it was only me who would possibly misconstrue those words, considering my ailment— as surely that was what it was—of always thinking with my dick when Carter was around. Keeping my mouth shut, I waited for some sort of response from him. His silence was unsettling; even more so was that he didn't snort at my words.

"I mean, you know, a shot of the hard stuff." I grimaced, pleased he couldn't see my heating face. Every time I said the word hard, I immediately thought of our cocks. "A whiskey or something? Bar?" I released a long breath as quietly as possible, waiting for him to answer.

Slowly, he turned, a smirk playing on his gorgeous mouth. With a small head tilt, his smirk grew to a smile. He then nodded. "Sure. That sounds good."

I gulped, trying not to think how fucking adorable he looked. I shook my head and glanced down at my clothes. I was dusty, with fragments of wood shavings on me from the day's work. "So, I'd best change, huh?"

Carter's gaze did a slow perusal of my body, seeming to take in every inch of me. Fuck, I'd spent too much time tossing off in the shower imagining the same thing but with us both naked. When his eyes flicked back to mine, he shook his head. "You look good enough to me."

My brows sprung high. "Okay." I shrugged, attempting to act unaffected. It was funny, despite our differences in work, his education, and upbringing, in comparison to my own, not once did I ever overthink the differences between us, or at least not too hard. Never did he ever make me feel as though we were on a different footing. And fuck, was it hard not to crush on him even harder because of it. I'd had a failed relationship in the past with a lawyer. It turned out he was an arrogant prick who took pleasure in telling his friends he was slumming it. It was no wonder I dumped his ass in record time once I'd overheard him; he'd been lucky I hadn't given him a black eye too.

But Carter was different, and my resolve to remain professional was a struggle. Our boundaries blurred, and I had to admit, I did wonder why I bothered putting the no-fraternizing rule in effect in the first place. I must have been on crack for sure. Would dating while working for him really screw it all up?

"So, where to?" he asked, interrupting my thoughts.

"Coleman's is a good spot." It was definitely a pub rather than a bar you'd find in the city. While it wasn't quite a sawdust floor, it was run-down and ancient, as were many of its locals. I'd been there several times, and it had fast become my favorite of the slim pickings in town. People were generally friendly; it was also where a few other tradesmen I'd met on other jobs hung out, plus it had a couple of pool tables and a dartboard.

"Sounds good." He grinned. The unhappiness from earlier still darkened his eyes, but the grin was definitely genuine. The small laughter lines around his eyes told me as much.

I cleared my throat, wondering how I'd reached the point of analyzing smiles and laughter lines. "I'll drive."

It was just ten minutes to the pub, which we rode in companionable silence. Carter had, I assumed, had a fucker of a day, and while I'd probably prod him later about what had gone on, I hoped he'd want to open up to me. Only time would tell.

The bar had a good crowd, not surprising for a Friday night. I indicated for Carter to grab a pool table while it was free, and I made my way to get our drinks. Rather than a whiskey, he asked for a gin and tonic. I'd smiled at his request and lifted my brows. It was a drink my mom had always called mother's ruin, simply because drinking too much led to emotional, drunken tears by the end of a session, so I'd smirked my way to order his drink, and got myself a bottle of Bud.

Carter had already racked up when I returned

with our drinks. I placed them on a small table to the side and took a swig of beer.

"Your break," Carter offered, handing me a cue.

"Sounds good." I threw him a wink as I took the cue and proceeded to break. It soon became clear that Carter was awful at the game, and he progressively became worse the more he drank. I also discovered he couldn't handle his gin.

But fuck, he was so funny and had genuine laughter bursting from my gut more than once. He was recounting a story from work involving a hamster, a snake, and a cat when his gaze was drawn to the opening door and the three men walking in. His laughter and story died off, his face paling.

Concern filled me when I looked at the men standing at the bar. I hadn't seen them around the place before, nor around town. They were in conversation while waiting for their drinks and seemed unaware of the impact they had on Carter. When I looked back at Carter, I walked over to him. He'd been in the process of taking a shot when he'd faltered and was since standing still and looking at the table. "Hey, where'd you go?"

He jumped at my voice, his unfocused gaze landing on mine. His wide eyes softened, his body relaxing a little when he released a breath. "Err, sorry. I think that last drink went to my head." His voice seemed strained, and he flicked his gaze over my shoulder, and no doubt toward the bar. I didn't fail to miss his clenched jaw. "Do you mind if we rain check this game and get out of here?" Once his eyes were back on mine, worry gnawed at my gut. I had no idea what was going on, but every nerve in my body was on edge, ready to step in and make sure Carter was okay.

I narrowed my eyes, not liking the thought that his reaction was one of fear. His piercing eyes begged me not to make a big deal of it though. They were focused, intent on mine, but slightly downcast. Everything in his body screamed he was desperate to leave, while mine roared that I wanted to head to the bar and those three guys to figure out what the fuck was going on.

Instead, I swallowed my need to bang heads and chose to do what he needed. "Sure thing. Let's get out of here."

Placing the cues down, Carter grabbed his jacket, and we made our way to the main doors. I positioned him to my right, closest to the wall and away from the bar, allowing him to be half a step ahead of me. As we angled to the exit, the three guys headed toward us, drinks in hand and seeming set on the pool table. Carter visibly tensed. I refocused my gaze on the men, all wearing slacks and button-up shirts, all looking ridiculously preppy.

One of the guys, who looked especially smooth, flared his nostrils when his eyes landed on Carter. A small sneer appeared on his face as though in distaste. Just as we passed, his not so quiet voice said, "Thank fuck the fags are leaving." I heard two snorts, one from the smooth fucker himself, and the other I assumed from one of his friends.

My reaction was immediate.

I spun on my heel, my face warming in anger, fist twitching and a curl of heat unfurling in my gut. "What the fuck?" My muscles clenched, wanting to pound into the hotshot's face. It wasn't the first time I'd heard a pathetic slur, and admittedly, in the past I hadn't necessarily lashed out in anger, but with Carter's anxiety, I was pretty sure caused by these guys, rational thought fled.

The fucker faced me. His lip curled again when his gaze flicked at Carter and then me. I stepped forward, relishing the waver of uncertainty that appeared on his face. The guy was all bravado. I knew with one fist to the face, he'd be on the ground, and I would take great pleasure in proving it.

"I said, what the fuck? You have something you want to say?"

His two friends turned in my direction, neither looking ready to square up to a fight or have their buddy's back. Anger pounded off me. I was sure each of the fuckers before me could feel it.

The preppy gulped, his eyes traveling to the right just as Carter's warm palm settled on my arm.

"Come on, Tanner. Let's just go." His voice was quiet, but I heard the tremor, felt it too.

My gaze remained on the guy before me, and I didn't miss the sneer he directed at Carter. I willed him to speak, to give me a reason to draw blood. Instead, he stayed silent.

"Thought as much." My voice was low, hard and demanding, immediately drawing his attention back to me. Carter released my arm and stepped slightly to the side. I turned to look at him. He was biting on his bottom lip, one I was desperate to draw into my mouth, and his cheeks carried a sexy blush. I unclenched my fist, reached out and took Carter's hand in mine.

On contact, he inhaled deeply, shock registering on his face, his cheeks warming even more. I gave his hand a light squeeze. "Come on, baby. Let's go." I didn't throw a warning glance over my shoulder as I left. That stupid fuck had got the message. Plus, with Carter's hand in mine, his skin heating my own, I didn't want to focus on anything or anyone but him. I just needed to get out of the bar before I shoved Carter against the wall in public to make it clear that the rules had changed.

Carter was going to be mine. Fuck the consequences.

CHAPTER EIGHT

CARTER

I WAS ON FIRE. MY SKIN THREATENED TO BURN OFF IN the best possible way. How on earth was that even a good thing? All I knew was when Tanner took on Scott, my heart had threatened to burst out of my chest with emotion for the man. He was strong and brave, and so goddamn sexy, and I wanted nothing more than to climb him like a freakin' tree and dry hump him.

Admittedly, I wanted to do that with him naked and him be inside me, but still, the intensity of my need threatened to have me clawing out of my skin. He was everything I wanted and never thought I'd have the chance to have.

His hand gripped mine as he tugged me out of the building, not stopping until we reached the car.

He unlocked it, pulled open the door, and ushered me in before getting himself settled and driving.

The silence was not the same as on the drive out. Tension pulsed between us. I was rock-hard, and I didn't want to shift or move for fear of breaking whatever spell had taken over us. I wanted him something fierce. After weeks of spending hours together, working side by side, eating and relaxing together, my desire for him was already heightened, but after the display in the bar, he'd gone and cata-pulted that desire to a supernova level of need.

I felt surprisingly sober after the anxiety that had swirled inside me when Scott had first entered. I'd been having such an amazing time with Tanner, finally unwinding after a nightmare of a day, caused by Scott Analson. His appearance over the past few weeks had caused lead to settle in my gut. It had seemed there was no escaping him or his cruel taunts, and having to deal with it outside of work was something I didn't think I could cope with— until Tanner had stepped in with his alpha delicious-ness. Scott retreating in on himself was a sight to behold. Not only did it set free a rush of justice, but it made me want Tanner even more. He'd said in not so many words that he wasn't interested in me. I'd respected that, hated it, but recognized it all the same. When his hand had taken mine into his strong, rough palm, though, that was when the fire had started, quickly turning into a raging inferno while in the car.

I had no idea what his plan was, or even if he had one. Damn, did I? I could step up and take charge when I needed or wanted to, but everything about Tanner cried control, and I wasn't necessarily thinking kinky stuff either. Though that did give me pause for thought. Tanner had, however, previously put his boundaries in place. It was up to him to change, move, or goodness, destroy the things completely. A guy could dream.

When we pulled up to my house, I turned my gaze to him. He gripped the steering wheel, his focus directly in front of him. After a few breaths, where I willed him to look at me, he stepped out of the car and walked around it.

The anticipation was killing me.

Realizing he was coming to the passenger door, I unbuckled my belt and made to open the door. I didn't have a chance. It was flung open, and Tanner filled the space.

The next moment I was in his arms and being ushered to the house. He pulled out his key, opened the door, and tugged me inside. Every second that slipped by left need pooling in my stomach and the desperate desire to have his mouth on mine. I hoped to God that was what he intended. I didn't think my heart or my constant hard-on could handle an alternative.

When the door closed behind us, Tanner finally turned and faced me. He backed me against the closed door, caging me in, his body a few inches from mine. With his hands flattened on either side of my head, his exhale brushed against my skin. My breath hitched at the nearness and intimacy.

I lifted my gaze to meet his; our eyes connected. I was sure mine widened when I took in the lust swirling there. My focus moved to his mouth, and I watched in delicious agony as his lips parted and he groaned. Flicking my eyes back to his, I bit back my own needy moan.

"Fuck, Carter." He closed his eyes when my name passed his lips. "I need to know you're okay."

Every muscle in my body tightened, and his eyelids sprung open. "What do you mean?" My voice was breathy, barely recognizable.

One of his arms shifted, his hand coming to my face, his fingers stroking my cheek. Relaxing into his touch, my lids dipped.

"I mean, are you okay from the bar?"

I was sure my heart stuttered at the concern in his voice. This man had the ability to snatch my heart, my soul away from me. I could only hope that he would take good care of it, as I was powerless to stop him even if I wanted to. Which I didn't.

I nodded. "Yes. I am now."

His fingers traveled to my mouth, and he ran the pads over my bottom lip. Tanner's gaze dropped there before rising back to mine.

"This changes everything."

I nodded again, desperate for his words to become my reality.

"And you're okay with that too?"

Heck, all I could do was keep nodding. I wanted the talking to stop, and I needed him to take me and make me his.

"Right answer." His large hand cupped my cheek, and he lowered his mouth to mine.

As his lips brushed against mine, I sighed in relief. The kiss was gentle, soft, not at all like the simmering passion sparking between us. But it was exactly as our first kiss should be.

Tanner's kisses drifted to my cheek, to my neck, and I angled for him, finally getting enough brain function to move my hands to touch him. Stroking his neck and trailing my fingers across his shoulders,

I angled my head to give him better access, loving the shivers shooting through me. My cock throbbed when his mouth went to my ear, and he lightly bit my lobe while his scruffy facial hair rubbed across my shaven skin. My hands found his hair and I brushed my fingers through the strands and held on to his head, tugging him nearer.

A rumble escaped his lips at my attention, and his mouth quickly found mine. Soft and gentle was gone, replaced with possession and need. Our lips pressed against each other's, Tanner's tongue delving into my mouth, finding my tongue and stroking it lightly. I thrust my groin against his at the action. He responded immediately, pressing his jean-clad erection against mine and deepening our kiss.

I needed more.

In tune, Tanner pulled away with a breathy groan. "Bed." It wasn't a question.

Smiling, I threw my arms around him and kissed him long and hard. He groaned once more, meeting my kisses with relish. Backing up a step, Tanner cupped my ass and squeezed. His hands felt so good and so right on me.

Eagerly, I pushed against him, not quite sure I had the willpower to make it to my bedroom. Needing more of him to see me through the next torturous thirty seconds before we found a mattress, or likely longer at the rate we were going, I ran a hand beneath his tee. The warmth of his skin was perfect under my touch. I caressed his back, reveling in his moans.

He tore his mouth from mine, making me stumble a moment before he gripped my ass once again and lifted me. "Fuck it," he murmured as my legs wrapped around him. He angled his head and planted a quick kiss on my lips before he spun us around and took long, confident strides to the staircase and all but charged upstairs.

I hung on for dear life, a complete mix of amused and turned on, and hoping like crazy he wouldn't drop me. At six foot, I was hardly light. Once in my room, he lowered me to the bed before standing and stripping naked.

With wide eyes, I watched every move, every drop of fabric as I reveled in the perfectness of Tanner. Tanned hard lines and angles greeted me, though I knew despite the firm muscles, his skin would be soft and welcoming.

"Keep looking at me like that, baby, and foreplay will be going right out the fucking window."

At his gravelly words, I locked eyes with his. Breathily, I answered, "I'm good with that." And oh my, was I! For weeks I'd dreamed of Tanner. What started as horny dreams of a hot body hadn't taken long to morph into passionate ones of a beautiful man with a kind soul.

A smile lit his face as he reached down and started the teasing process of removing my clothes.

CHAPTER NINE

TANNER

Fuck. Carter was fucking perfect.

Somehow I'd held back from tearing off his clothes and slamming into him. Our combined need was heady. From a build-up of weeks' worth of pent-up desire and attraction to finally shrugging off the ridiculous logic of why we shouldn't just give in, I was ready to explode and bury myself balls deep in him.

There was no fucking way I was doing that. We'd waited too long. I needed to savor every caress, to enjoy the taste of him. And more than that, I needed to unravel him before I took possession and made him mine.

I was under no illusions. With the friendship we'd built and our instant and growing attraction, there was no way a quick fuck or even one fuck would be enough. I hadn't even tasted him, yet I knew that soul deep.

Speaking of tasting, I licked his shaft, savoring the velvet-soft skin covering the hardness. Carter groaned as I made my way toward his balls and took the time to suck and lick, pulling each one into my mouth.

"Harder," he gasped. "Yes, like that," he grunted as I tugged his sac.

My dick throbbed at his words, his reaction, knowing how good it felt. Releasing a ball with a pop, I looked up at him as I trailed hot kisses along his shaft. His eyes were on me, drifting between my mouth and my eyes. When I then licked over the head, circling and paying attention to his sensitive slit, his eyes squeezed shut, and he threw his head back.

"Please, Tanner."

I grinned just before I wrapped my mouth around him. With one hand gripping the base, I bobbed my head repeatedly, hollowing my cheeks as I sucked. He groaned again, urging me to take him as deep as possible. I moved both hands to his ass. With a palm on each butt cheek for leverage, I tugged him toward me; his cock hit the back of my throat. I concentrated on breathing, on making him fall apart so that he would never want another man but me near him again.

He gasped as I pulled back to twirl my tongue around him and placed soft open-mouthed kisses on his damp skin. Just before I took him in deep, I maneuvered my other hand to his mouth. He opened immediately and sucked the two digits I offered. Satisfied, I removed my fingers and edged them toward his puckered hole and dipped one in. His hand found my face as he stroked my cheek, his eyes once more on me. Carefully pushing past his tight ring of muscle, I swirled my finger around, pumping in and out before pulling out and dipping a second in along with the first.

"Oh my God." His words were a garbled gasp as I plunged into him and sucked him off, my fingers and mouth working in harmony. I wanted him to explode, wanted to taste every drop of him and suck him dry.

Pressing into him deeper, harder, I stroked his prostate. Carter groaned, and his hips jerked out of control. In response, I hollowed my cheeks harder and continued to press against him. Bobbing my head, I glanced up, desperate to see his expression. His eyes were at half-mast, his lower lip caught between his teeth. He'd never looked fucking sexier.

Driving harder over him, I watched as he groaned, mumbling, "Yes," over and over. "I'm going to come," he warned. I would have grinned if my mouth hadn't been filled with his perfection. With a couple more bobs of my head, my tongue stroking the underside of his shaft, hot, salty shots of cum sprayed into my mouth, most hitting my throat.

Moaning around him, I knew the rumble would be felt deeply. He jerked as if on cue, his eyes widening. All the time I sucked and licked, not wanting to waste a single drop. I'd done this to him. Made him lose control and come hard.

Pulling back, I took him in my hand and proceeded to lick him clean, my hand stroking him. Ripples of shock still shook his body, and when my gaze locked on his, a smile lit his face.

"I need you inside me." Carter's thumb traced my bottom lip while he spoke. "So fucking bad it hurts."

I grinned. It was the first time I'd heard a serious cuss escape his lips. It was hot that he lost control and let his guard down. My heartbeat picked up speed knowing I was moments away from having him wrapped around me and that he was so acutely affected that he'd shared a part of him I'd never seen before. Then I kissed my way up his body. With my lips on his, I pried his mouth open with a slip of my tongue. He took me in, his arms enfolding me while our lips moved against each other. Breaking the kiss gently took all my willpower, but my need was too strong. I nibbled on his bottom lip before adjusting myself on my knees.

"Do you want me to turn over?" he asked.

I shook my head. "No, I want to see you when I take you."

He shuddered at my words, that blush I loved so much covering his cheeks.

"Nightstand." His words were quiet and breathy.

Reaching over to the nightstand, I opened the drawer and took hold of a foil wrapper and some lube. As I positioned the covering, Carter's eyes followed my hands. His breathing picked up speed as he moved his legs, positioning his feet flat on the mattress. Squirting the lube on my fingers, I rubbed it over my covered shaft and then reached out to him.

I took the time to caress his balls first, while I bobbed in excitement as I watched his pupils dilate. Then I rubbed my fingers gently over his diamond, knowing his prostate was already swollen with desire. He gasped at the contact, his cock jerking, already almost fully erect. Pulling my bottom lip between my teeth, I ran my fingers to his puckered hole and dipped in. He was tight from his orgasm and perfect. With two fingers, I spent time preparing him while my right hand caressed his stomach and then landed on his shaft.

Carter moved his hips, riding my fingers, the movement sliding his shaft through my grip. "No, baby. Please. Fuck me."

With my need too great, I was unable to manage a smile at his desperate pleas and the hot-as-fuck cussing. Instead, I removed my fingers, edged forward, grabbed a pillow, and placed it beneath his hips. He sighed at the loss but eagerly lifted his legs for me, willing me to drive into him. Placing myself at the entrance, I dipped in and out gently, taking my time. Satisfied with his eagerness, I tortured both of us by easing into him painfully slowly. He was lubed, wet, and eager as he jerked his hips impatiently.

"Fuck," I ground out as the action planted me deeper inside him, way past the tight ring. Sliding out slightly, I then bucked my hips, going in further, but still not balls deep. My muscles shook under the pressure of holding back while my breath caught in my chest.

"Tanner, please," Carter whimpered.

I pulled back once more, then slammed into him. Both of us cried out. Our eyes locked. This time my grin came easily as I absorbed the lust painting his face. "Perfect." I bit the words out as I built a steady rhythm entering him and withdrawing. With each movement, my balls drew tighter.

Needing to see his own lust heighten, I ordered, "Touch yourself." He did so immediately. My gaze traveled between his entrance, his hand, and his face, not wanting to miss out on any moment or sight, each one uniquely hot. Moving my hand to his, I helped jerk him off while continuing to bury myself deep inside him.

It was becoming harder to concentrate on anything but the sensation of being wrapped up in him, or the building orgasm. I was set to combust, my cock painfully hard. "Come for me, baby." I moved my hand harder as my hips lurched, needing to see his cum.

He released a strangled cry, and I continued jerking him off, plowing into him at the same time. Finally, white ropes spurted out of him, landing on my hand and his stomach. I groaned and came hard, growling out his name as lightness spread throughout my body, curling my toes. Each muscle tensed, and I shuddered, my eyes on the jets of white spread over our joined hands. And then finally, my gaze settled on his face.

With pink cheeks and a smile ghosting his lips, he'd never looked more handsome. *Perfect.*

―――――

I woke to the scent of coffee and the mattress dipping. I turned my head and pried open my eyes. Carter had just set two mugs of coffee down and was climbing back into bed, completely unaware of me watching him.

With a grin, I reached out to him and snagged his waist, tugging him to me.

With an oomph and a high-pitched squeal that caused a laugh to burst out of my chest, I grinned at him. He sprawled over me, cheeks pink and eyes wide. Then he frowned. "Are you laughing at me?"

Another burst of laughter erupted, which quickly turned to a yelp when he twisted my nipple. "Fuck, baby, you're making me hard." I pressed my hard-on against him to prove my point, loving the O that appeared on his lips.

He gulped before a small smirk crept onto his mouth. "Morning."

I pulled his face to mine. "Morning," I replied before we kissed.

By the time my tongue was in his mouth and caressing his, something he really seemed to like, he was straddling me and grinding his erection against mine. His lips then broke free. "Hey," I said. "Back here."

Carter raised his brows, a flirtatious smile on his mouth. "Oh. If you'd prefer my lips on your morning wood, I can do that." He shrugged indifferently as if he couldn't see or feel said wood doing a fucking hula dance at the mere mention of a blow job.

I gripped his ass and squeezed. "I'm happy for you to put your lips anywhere on my body, baby. Anytime."

He grinned at my words and gave me a chaste kiss. My heart constricted. I'd never had this before. This connection. I'd thought I'd had something similar in the past, but that had been a one-night stand that had simply continued for over a year. My wiser, older self would have known that particular relationship would never have worked, but what Carter and I potentially had was already so much more.

"Anytime, huh?"

I nodded and moved my hands to tuck them behind my head, elbows up and out. "That's right."

"You know, I may just have to test that theory."

Smiling at Carter, I happily admitted to myself that I liked this side of him, a lot. The playful banter with a dangerous edge of "I may just let you fuck me if you play your cards right." Yeah, it was hot.

"Sounds like a challenge I'm happy to let you win," I said with a smirk.

He glanced to the side and then back at me. "I also made you coffee."

I couldn't usually function without coffee in the morning, but it seemed Carter was a new caffeine-free pick-me-up. I had no problem functioning with Carter straddling me and offering me his mouth.

"Let it go cold." My voice dipped in eager anticipation. "And get your mouth on mine." I needed that even more than I needed to be inside his mouth. Who the fuck would have thought it?

His mouth was on mine in an instant. Our lips met, mouths parting. When I wrapped my arms around Carter and pulled him closer, I knew I could happily start every day like this.

Heat spread through me, and I lost myself in the touch of his mouth, the feel of his skin, and the rightness that settled in my chest.

CHAPTER TEN

CARTER

It was no surprise I was not looking forward to Monday morning. The thought of seeing Scott again and the possible repercussions of what transpired Friday night left an unsavory taste in my mouth and my gut clenching in dread.

"Hey, what's going on in that head of yours?" Tanner pressed his lips against my brow, a gesture that seemed surprisingly natural.

For the past twenty-four hours, we'd been living in a world of heat and connection. Lost in each other's bodies, we'd spent the morning after the bar debacle pretty much in bed. I'd been quietly terrified when I'd woken in Tanner's arms, worried that things would be awkward. Nothing could have been further from that, thank God.

We'd fallen into easy roles, not that dissimilar to our connection of the past couple of months, but this time with the delectable bonus of kisses and cocks. I grinned at the thought, despite the turmoil of work.

"Just thinking about work tomorrow." I'd yet to share the details of Scott with Tanner, instead welcoming his touches and reveling in getting lost in comfortable conversation.

He shifted on the sofa, so I was forced to look at him. A frown dipped his brows. "What's the problem with work?"

Releasing a heavy sigh, I knew it was time to tell him what had been going on the past few weeks. The reality was, I was embarrassed. I was a grown-ass man, a professional at that, yet I was still dealing with ridiculousness at work. The word bullying flitted through my consciousness, yet I brushed it aside. I wasn't a kid anymore, and it certainly wasn't high school. But still, ever since Denver had left, leaving his godson in charge, my life had plummeted right back into a time I'd hated, a time filled with bigotry and harassment. The difference was at high school—after I'd been unceremoniously outed by a few asshole jocks—I'd had a ray of light at the end of my nightmare, knowing that high school would eventually end. I'd just had to survive the final three months before graduating and leaving for college. But this was my life, my profession. Short of leaving a job I loved, I could no longer see a ray of light.

"Tell me."

I nodded, knowing I would hate the tremble in my voice that would no doubt lace my words when I spoke. Regardless, I pushed on. I could trust Tanner with this. "That guy from Friday night."

"The prick?"

I nodded, a smirk tilting my mouth despite my nerves. "That's Scott."

Tanner tilted his head, his eyes tightening before he spoke. "The guy who's taken over for your boss?"

I nodded again. I'd already told him briefly about what had been happening at work with the changeover. Obviously over dinner the past few weeks, I'd neglected to share with him exactly what had been going on.

He reached out and placed his hand on my forearm. "Tell me."

I watched his jaw clench, understanding he was pissed off on my behalf. I would have been lying if the knowledge didn't stir a lightness in my chest, the first I'd felt about work since Scott had started making my life miserable.

"When Denver was around the first week, everything was fine. Well, sort of. Things with Scott were a bit, I don't know, awkward." I shrugged. I'd just brushed it aside as an uptight personality and his nerves at stepping up to run the place. He'd been thrown into the deep end, so I'd assumed it was just the stress of the situation.

"Then what happened?"

"It started off as little things, a few 'jokey' comments thrown my way about liking dick and the 'fags' in a new TV show." I'd held my own often, laughing along, even throwing it back, and trying to shut him down about how inappropriate he was being. "It wasn't until a couple of weeks ago that I noticed more and more cancellations with some of my more regular clients, you know, weekly injections, even a couple of operations." I glanced at Tanner's thumb as he rubbed it over my arm in soothing circles and then I took a breath, appreciating how the slightest attention gave me the added boost to continue.

"I mentioned it to Lauren, who said she'd noticed it too. She actually checked it out for me, and last week, she told me that each cancellation had actually been swapped to an appointment with Scott."

Tanner's hand stilled. "What the fuck? He's stealing clients from you?"

I shrugged again. "I had no idea what to think, so I went and asked him. At first he shrugged it off saying he had nothing to do with the bookings, but then the next day I saw Mrs. Carson heading out after an appointment, which she'd previously had with me. When I said hi, she seemed surprised to see me, letting me know that her appointment had been changed to Dr. Anderson since I was on a research project and was having to hand over my clients."

When she'd told me, my grin had frozen in place. It took her asking me if I was okay to bring me out of my daze before I'd smiled politely and excused myself. I'd immediately sought out Scott and asked for an explanation.

I shook my head. "He said he'd had a few complaints and requests to change to him, and that he then thought it best that he change some of my longstanding appointments while he investigated further." Heat rushed to my cheeks at the memory. I'd been as shocked as I was annoyed, so much so I'd just stood there like a freakin' goober trying to make sense of everything before he'd ushered me out as he had another client.

"On Friday, I finally approached him and asked for an explanation."

Tanner's voice was low when he asked, "What happened?" The skin around his eyes was tight, his own cheeks flushed as he waited intently for me to finish.

"He told me that it was clear 'my kind' wasn't welcome in the practice or even the town, and that it had already cost Denver business." It was bullcrap. I knew it and had argued as much, my anger rising at the need to defend myself. "He made it clear that 'fags' were better off in places where 'civilized citizens' weren't the backbone of the town."

Tanner sprung off the sofa just as I finished speaking, his half-nakedness not even distracting me from the rage present in his voice and his tense muscles. "I'm going to fucking kill him. The piece of shit…"

He spun around, still rambling and cussing. He grabbed his shirt from the floor.

"…if that fucker thinks he can speak to you…"

It was tugged on as I remained on the sofa, wide-eyed in shock. I'd never had anyone defend me before—not counting my parents. My chest squeezed tightly and a lump caught in my throat.

"…his address?"

My eyes shot to his. Having not really heard a word he said, I had no idea how to react. All I wanted was to drag him toward me and hold him close. His defense, his reaction... it meant everything.

"Carter, his address?"

There was no chance I was telling him he lived just a few doors away. I was just relieved that Tanner had never spotted him. I shook my head and bit my bottom lip. His gaze fell to my mouth, and he took two steps forward until his legs pressed to the side of the sofa.

I clambered to my knees and scooted forward, reaching out and pressing my palm against his bare chest. My lips quickly replaced my hand. His breath caught, and his pecs twitched. Smiling lightly, I continued my ministrations, luxuriating in the taste of his skin, the feel of his hardening nipple in my mouth.

"Address, Carter. You're not going to distract me."

I didn't believe him and knew that he didn't believe his words either as his large palm cupped the back of my head and he angled my face up to him.

Our eyes locked and my breathing increased when I stared at the beautiful man before me. He'd quickly become my everything. Even before the past twenty-four hours, he was firmly placed in my life, but since we'd finally opened ourselves to something more, I had no hesitation in admitting to myself that Tanner could quite possibly be *it*.

"Kiss me."

His gaze darkened, lust swirling in his gray eyes.

"Tanner, I need you to kiss me."

A low growl escaping from his lips was my warning. His mouth slammed on mine, our lips, our breaths, our tongues clashing, melding, urging for more. With every stroke and caress of his tongue, I whimpered. I needed him inside me, taking me, connecting us in a way so deep that no words, no bigotry, no one from outside this moment could stop me from seeing how perfect Tanner was for me.

In a matter of seconds, Tanner was once again naked. Our lips still connected, I released a surprised squeal when he lifted me, carried me to my bedroom and placed me on the bed. A moment later, he lay on the mattress and pulled me on top of him.

"I need to see." His voice was breathy, filled with desire.

I nodded in understanding and reached over for the lube and condom. His eyes drifted from my face, our erections, and my hand; it was obvious that he wished he could focus on all three at once. When I rolled the condom on though, he surprised me by focusing on my eyes.

"You know how much I want you, need you?" His eyes were surprisingly hard when he spoke, as though urging me to truly understand every syllable he spoke and believe them.

"Yes," I answered with a nod. With my eyes fixed on his, I slathered lube on his sheathed erection and reached to my entrance. I gasped on touch, eager for Tanner to fuck me.

A grin broke free on his perfect mouth, lifting the dangerous edge from his eyes. "Good. Now put your cock in my mouth."

I groaned and didn't even have time to respond before he clamped his big palms on my ass and shifted me up to his face. He lifted his head and angled me the way he wanted before his tongue dipped out and licked the tip of my glans, focusing on lapping up my precum.

When he took me in his mouth, a loud cry rushed out of me. "Holy fuck." I jerked my hips, encouraging him to take me deeper, despite the awkward position. Tanner pulled back after a few sucks and licked me once more, his eyes lifting to mine as his fingers slid down my crease. I didn't hold back the delicious shudder that racked my body. Biting my lip, painfully desperate for him, but not wanting to change this moment for anything, I gasped when he circled my tight opening. Already I pulsed, knowing how good it would feel when I was wrapped around him.

His voice was rough and the deepest it had ever been when he spoke. "One day I'm going to prepare you with my tongue. Fuck, baby, I can't wait." His finger pushed through my entrance, and I leaned back against him in wonder. Never had I been rimmed, and hell if the thought of Tanner doing something so primal, so fucking forbidden didn't have my balls drawing up. "You want that?"

I nodded my response as he pushed in farther, this time stretching me with two fingers. "Oh my God!" My words were gravelly, desperate. "I can't...." I needed him inside me, wanted him there before I exploded.

Tanner removed his fingers immediately, scooted me back, and pulled my lips to his. Our mouths met with a ferocity we'd yet to share, surprising since every connection had seemed just that. I groaned, his mouth capturing the sound, before I leaned away and positioned myself above him.

I sank down carefully, feeling the delicious burn.

I winced despite loving every inch that filled me. Catching my hips with his rough hands, Tanner forced me to pause.

"You good?"

I smirked. "Perfect."

He searched my eyes momentarily before releasing his grip, and I sank lower before easing myself up and lowering once more. When I finally pressed against him as far as I could go, deep and resting against my skin, he took my hands in his. Our fingers laced together, and I used his strength, his toned arms as support and leverage. Tentative at first, not knowing if he would support my weight and movement, I grinned, realizing there was never a need to have doubted him.

From everything that I had discovered about Tanner over the past two months, I was certain of many things. Not only was he steadfast and kind, but I knew without hesitation, he would not let me fall.

CHAPTER ELEVEN

TANNER

AFTER STEPPING OUT OF THE SHOWER, I SMILED AT Carter, lightly snoring. I'd struggled to sleep so had already snuck away at the ass-crack of dawn and done some work in one of the bedrooms. It had been a particularly dirty couple of hours involving dust, drywall, and paint. Admittedly, I hadn't been fully concentrating, still brooding and wanting to take action against Scott.

I looked at the time and knew Carter's alarm would go off in ten minutes. He had been just as restless when we'd first headed to bed. While he'd appeared relieved to have finally shared the bullcrap he'd been through over the past few weeks, his anxiety had spiked, and unfortunately, I was the cause.

He was genuinely terrified I was going to kick Scott's ass.

And fuck, did I want to.

The thought of anyone intimidating him, making him feel like crap, and hurting him in any way had my blood boiling. Hell, every time my thoughts drifted in that direction I wanted to go on a rampage. I didn't think a simple ass-kicking would do it though. I wanted to rip the fucker's head off.

Carter shifted in the bed, his light snore stopping, and I released my tight jaw and exhaled. How anyone could attack him was beyond me. Carter was one of the sweetest guys I knew. He was kind and thoughtful, and I was sure he didn't have a mean bone in his body. The fact that Scott had gone after him by challenging his position at work and possibly destroying his career was all sorts of fucked-up. Carter loved his job, loved helping animals, and indirectly their owners. There was no chance ever I'd be allowing the godawful harassment to continue.

While I wanted to march into the clinic with guns blazing, I knew that would distress Carter even more. I needed to use my smarts to help and protect him. I just hadn't quite figured out exactly what that would consist of yet.

"Hey." Carter's gruff voice drew my attention to him. With ruffled hair and eyes not yet fully open, he looked sexy as hell. My feet reacted immediately. I was beside the bed in a few strides and then leaning down and kissing him.

"Morning," I said as I pulled away, brushing wayward hair out of his eyes.

He released a happy sigh and grinned up at me. "You been up long? You should have woken me for a shower." His smile turned mischievous.

I laughed, ignoring my hard-on jerking in agreement. "You need to get up and prepare for work. No way would we have long enough if we'd showered together, not when I'm considering all the things I want to do with you in the shower." I lifted my brows a few times and beamed even harder at the flush that rose in his cheeks. I would never get tired of seeing the pink spreading across his skin.

"I suppose you're right." He reached to the bedside table and took hold of his phone, pressing a few digits.

"You get ready, and I'll start breakfast." I still wanted to talk to him before he went to work. I suspected it was the last thing he wanted to do, but I couldn't sit by while he suffered. I reached down, took hold of his hands, and tugged him up and out of bed. He ended up flush with my body, and it was impossible to not admit just how perfectly he fit.

Placing a chaste kiss on his lips as opposed to pressing hard and taking control of the kiss like my body demanded, I squeezed his ass and gave a gentle slap.

A squeak-groan escaped his parted lips. Fuck, this guy was dangerous. Dipping toward the crease of his neck, I placed a light kiss there and then inhaled. The scent of sex and Creed, the aftershave I'd quickly become addicted to over the past month, filled me. He smelled delicious. "Shower," I murmured before turning and heading to the safety of the kitchen.

Ten minutes later, we sat down to coffee and toast. I was nothing if not a food connoisseur. I allowed him a bite and a sip before I just plowed straight in. "I'll drop you off at work today." Carter paused midchew, his eyes narrowing slightly before his shoulders dropped. "I'm not going to say or do anything, but the BS needs to stop." It was a half-assed attempt to reassure him.

Swallowing hard, he took a gulp of coffee, wincing at the heat. "I know you mean well, and don't get me wrong, you sounding macho and going all gung-ho is making me hard"—it was my turn to narrow my eyes at him. I wasn't fucking about with this—"but I've tried. I made it clear that I knew what he was up to, which resulted in nothing but contempt. And what else exactly am I supposed to do, short of either ignoring it or leaving? He's the boss for at least another couple of months. There's no one else to talk to. He *is* the management."

I hated the defeat in his voice just as much as I understood his logic and position. "There has to be something. Are you in some kind of union or something? How about contacting his uncle—"

"Godfather."

"—godfather then? No one has the right to say or to do the things he's doing. It's not right. You love your job. You can't let this fucker drive you out. I won't allow it." My voice had gradually become louder as I spoke, anger and frustration fueling my words.

Carter reached out and placed his palm on my forearm. "Thank you." I quirked my head in question. "For caring, for wanting to make things better and right for me." His blush was back. "It actually really helps that you know. I don't feel as, I don't know, alone in the whole thing." He cleared his throat as he flicked his gaze away briefly before settling back on me. "These past few weeks have been pretty dire, with last Friday being the worst of it." My muscles flexed under his palm, causing him to grip me and then draw soothing circles on my skin with his thumb.

"You being here when I get home from work, us spending time with each other, being friends"—I made to speak, wanting to make it clear that after this weekend we were a lot more than that, but he stopped me with a grin—"and now becoming... us"—my cock twitched and stomach tensed at the word. I liked it a lot—"well, it makes everything that's happening at work seem insignificant. Helped me get into work, do my job, and switch off from Scott."

I loved giving that to him. Every word he spoke felt right, and I'd be lying if his belief in what we were just starting with each other didn't make my chest puff out with pride. Yet, it was not okay for him to have to "put up" with the harassment. "But that's the point." I took his hands in mine. "It's not insignificant, and he's ruining something you love. You can't let him get away with any of it. It needs to stop." I meant every word. While I didn't attend LGBT rallies or anything, I still fought for human rights and equality. That didn't mean I waved a flag around—though if I did, I would rock that shit—but it did mean if I heard someone talking crap or behaving like an asshole, I had no hesitation in calling them out for it.

Carter dipped his head forward. I knew it was so easy for me to point out the rights and wrongs, the injustices in the world, and demand that it stop and he do something about it. It was a lot more complicated than that. But just because life could be harsh and difficult didn't mean that anyone, especially Carter, should have to put up with harassment or being pushed out of his job. He had to fight for this.

"Hey." I released one of his hands and lifted his chin so our eyes connected. "Whatever you need, I'll support you, okay? You don't have to deal with any of this alone." I waited for what felt like a lifetime as the air around us crackled with tension. The slightest of nods from Carter though had me exhaling deeply. I grinned, a big-ass genuine smile. "I've got your back."

He nodded again. "Thanks, Tanner."

Our gazes remained locked before I dragged my eyes away, conscious of the time. "Come on. Best get your fine ass to work." I stood and tugged him up with me. "I'm driving." I grabbed my keys and pulled him toward the door, not giving him a chance to stop me. "You have everything you need?" I asked before we stepped outside.

He picked up his wallet and jacket before nodding. "I do now." Once outside, he paused. "Oh, lunch."

"Don't worry, I'll bring you some." I caught his blush and pleased grin as he stepped toward the car door. "Yeah, yeah, not only can I toast bread, I can make a mean sandwich."

Carter snorted. "I look forward to it."

The car journey, while quiet, was surprisingly relaxed. I was expecting Carter to be agitated, so I was impressed he was taking everything in his stride. He was no pushover; gentle, sure, but he wasn't weak, nor was he a pussy. Because of that, I'd had a hard time this past weekend trying to get my head around the situation with Scott.

I supposed I was lucky and hadn't really found myself in that situation. Even as a teenager, I'd been a big guy. I'd also been openly gay. I knew mine was a rare story; I hadn't been bullied or ridiculed in high school, or even during my apprenticeship. It helped that I had a reputation for handling myself as well as being a cocky fucker, and that two of my best friends, both straight, in addition to Davis who was bi had known for as long as I had that only guys did it for me.

We were a bunch of jerkoff jocks, all four of us. My attitude, good arm, and kickass friends had meant I'd been protected and pretty untouchable. Sure, over the years, I'd received stares, some disgusted glances or double takes when I'd been holding hands with a guy. There had also been a fucktard or five who thought it would be a riot to shout fag or whatever unimaginative crap they came up with at me. But each and every time was an isolated moment, not even an incident.

I knew I was lucky, just as I knew I'd been an arrogant fuck. But what I also knew was that most weren't as lucky as me. And that sucked like ass.

"What time shall I bring lunch?" I asked as we pulled up outside the clinic.

Carter angled toward me and smiled. "Are you going to eat with me and we can have a lunch date?" He wiggled his brows suggestively. "You know you don't have to woo me, right?"

I arched a brow at him return. "Woo you? What fucking century have you just stepped out of? Seriously? Woo?" I teased.

Leaning toward me, his eyes squinting in what I

was assuming was meant to be pissed or intimidating, he said, "Yes, woo. It's a word. People use it."

My laughter filled the small space of the car. "Yes, I'm aware it's a word, dork."

He pressed his hand against my chest. I couldn't help but flex under his palm. And there it was. The pink. "Dork?"

"Yes, dork. I like dorks, so it's all good." I took his hand in mine and tugged him close. "Now what time do you want me to woo you?"

His grin was perfect. I'd done the right thing taking him to work. I wanted him to start on a positive at least. "Midday works."

My lips touched his. "Good," I mumbled before pulling back. "Just get through today, yeah? We'll figure things out tonight." I pressed my forehead to Carter's, hating that my words brought him back to reality.

"Okay." He then moved away and got out of the car. I swiftly followed suit. Carter paused, looking over at me. "What are you doing?"

I shrugged nonchalantly. "Just walking you in."

"Tanner…."

"You can show me where you'll be so I'll know how to find you later."

Carter nibbled on his bottom lip. "You can just let

whoever is on reception know you're here. They'll get me."

"Nope." I stepped forward, took hold of his hand and led him toward the door to the clinic. "That won't do. I need the visual. It'll help with my fantasies later when I feel the urge to jack off when I should be working. My boss is a ballbreaker." Carter snorted and shoulder-checked me lightly. "But I gotta say, he's kinda hot. He's the reason I have to take my hand to myself at least a couple of times a day."

I turned to look at him and grinned at his wide eyes and gaping mouth. "What?" I asked. "I'm kinda hoping after this weekend, that I'll find the need less and less."

"I—" Carter cleared his throat. "I'm sure that we can figure something out." A playful glint entered his eyes when he paused, and his gaze roamed my face. "The last thing we want to happen is your job to be affected as you've developed carpal tunnel."

My heart squeezed and my gut clenched, right alongside the jerking taking place in my pants. Mischievous Carter was my favorite. Well, after sexy Carter. "Come on." I tugged on his hand and then reached over and opened the door, holding it ajar for him.

I allowed Carter to lead me inside, hand still in mine.

———

I WASN'T INTO LABELS, BUT I KNEW I WAS HAPPY spending as much time with Carter as possible. In and out of the sheets. On my drive back to his place, I caught myself smirking.

I was okay to admit to myself that holding his hand as we walked into the clinic had felt right. I was even more okay to admit that when I'd kissed him, just a small press of my lips against his in the doorway of the staff room, I'd found it surprisingly hard to pull away and leave it at that.

When I had pulled away, albeit reluctantly, I'd brushed my thumb across his bottom lip. It was then that his new boss had appeared in the corridor. My attention had been drawn immediately to him. My grip had flexed instinctively on Carter's waist and caused a small noise to escape from his lips.

I'd focused back on Carter immediately, wondering how he would handle the situation. I'd been relieved that his eyes were on me, and while his cheeks had flushed, the emotion playing on his features wasn't fear or anxiety. Instead, confidence was evident. It was there in the sparkle in his eyes, the slight curve of his mouth.

I'd grinned, pressed my lips to his once more, and then pulled away saying, "I'll see you at noon. Be good." I'd winked before turning and heading down the corridor, directly toward Scott. I'd sought out his eyes, willing him to say something that would give me a reason to punch him. He'd remained silent, his jaw clenched and his eyes straight ahead after a brief flick to mine.

"Morning," I'd offered with a smirk on my face.

He'd cleared his throat but didn't say anything. A slight bob of his head the only acknowledgment I received. My grin had grown wider, and before I turned the corner, which would lead me to the reception, I cast a glance over my shoulder to see Carter watching me, and Scott gone. I'd thrown Carter a wink before I'd headed out, thoroughly pleased with how that had gone down.

A few minutes later I pulled up at Carter's. I had a heap of tasks to get through, but I also wanted to make sure I left myself enough time to sort lunch and do a bit of research. I needed to offer Carter some solutions. He was a smart guy, fuck, a helluva lot smarter than me, and I was sure he'd thought about employee rights and laws, but I hoped if I had some insight then I'd be able to give him the boost in courage needed to see this through.

I just hoped I could understand the thing. Only time would tell.

Meanwhile, I got my ass into gear and continued in one of the spare bedrooms. One of the walls had needed ripping out and drywalling. The others had been in pretty good shape, better than I hoped, which would save Carter a bit of cash.

I paused at the thought, screwdriver in hand. Fuck. Since we were together—yeah, we hadn't used a term, but as far as I was concerned he was mine— how the fuck did everything work? I groaned, hating the spike in my adrenaline. It was the key reason I'd tried to keep my distance by not wanting to start anything. I scoffed. *Look at how well that worked out, asshole.*

I cracked my neck, urging rational thought to my brain. I detested having to take money from him to fix up his house, but then, as I glanced around the room and considered everything that needed to be done, the reality was it wasn't as simple as a paint job or even fitting a kitchen. It was months' worth of work. We'd agreed on the price, and I had no choice but to follow through. While I'd love nothing more than to be able to step up and be all chivalrous and shit, I had rent and bills to pay. Life would be easier once I finally sold my old place, which was almost complete. In the meantime, not wanting to accept payment was something that I'd have to get over.

An irritating voice in my head whispered the possibility of everything going haywire, but I refused to think of that as an option. Admittedly we'd had just a weekend together, but we'd had a couple of months of spending time with each other virtually every day. There were many things I was sure of in my life and my growing feelings for Carter were just a few among them.

CHAPTER TWELVE

CARTER

I'D WALKED PAST SCOTT TWICE SO FAR THIS MORNING, and I didn't even receive a sneer. I took that as a win, but it did little to ease the tension sitting in my gut or in my shoulders. I wondered whether Tanner would be up to giving me a massage when I got home. I smirked at the thought as I stirred sugar into my coffee.

"It's all the talk, you know."

I turned and looked at Lauren.

"You and the hottie." She headed to the fridge, pulled out some creamer, and then made her way over to me.

I kept my face neutral. "Hottie?" I asked and blew on my coffee.

"No pleading ignorance. Spill." She turned

squiny eyes at me, ones I assumed were meant to be intimidating.

My lips curved and formed into a wide smile. It was impossible not to when I thought about my weekend. "That would be Tanner."

Her eyes widened, and a dirty grin appeared on her face. "You sly dog. The guy who's doing up your place?"

I nodded. "One and the same."

"And now doing you apparently!" She laughed loudly, and I snorted hard.

I took a quick glance at the clock. I still had five minutes before my next appointment. So far I'd had no cancellations either, so I assumed it was all good. I took a seat while Lauren made herself a drink.

"So handholding and sweet kisses." A light sigh escaped her lips. "When did this all happen? 'Cause, I gotta say, I'm pissed you didn't tell me, and damn, you said he was good-looking, but, Carter, you've been holding out on me. He's smoking, and... did you see his muscles?"

I grinned and nodded again. I'd spent countless hours licking every single inch of his body over the weekend and knew every muscle the man possessed. I'd become pretty fond of one in particular, the one that made me chant and scream his name. I closed my eyes at the thought, willing myself to behave and not react. "I didn't realize you'd seen him this morning," I countered, needing to brush aside any talk of Tanner's delectable body. "Where were you?"

"Oh, I was there. I had just pulled up when you headed inside. I may have rushed and got my jacket caught in the car door." She laughed. "But heck, I needed to see what was going on. In all the time we've known each other, I've never known you to date. It's just so amazing." She reached out her hand and squeezed mine as she sat.

Warmth settled over me like a welcome blanket. While Lauren could be a bit full-on at times, her heart was always in the right place. "Hell, you're excited. I'm freakin' ecstatic," I admitted. She was the closest friend I'd had since moving, so while I still kept many cards close to my chest, there were some areas in my life I willingly gushed over. Tanner was one of those.

"So are you guys serious?"

I chuckled. "Geez, Lauren, it's been one weekend of hotness."

"I know," she interrupted, "but you've known him for a while now, right? And seem to spend a lot of time with the guy."

Nodding, I contemplated how exactly to describe

my relationship with Tanner. "Yeah, we do spend most evenings and some weekends together. And heck, I like him a lot. This past weekend was incredible. I'm not sure we're ready to put a name on it though." The thought of having that conversation with him made my stomach dip. There was no way to look cool or even at ease when asking "Will you go steady with me?" I internally groaned at the embarrassment to come.

"Yeah, I get it. So tell me, how'd it finally happen?"

I hadn't told Lauren the extremity of the situation with Scott. While she was aware of the appointment issue, she hadn't witnessed any of the vileness that he'd thrown my way. I'd kept that quiet, not wanting to cause a ripple. In just a month or so, Denver would be back so Scott would be out of there, and everything would be just fine.

I shrugged noncommittally. "We had a couple of drinks Friday night, and the rest fell into place."

"Or Tanner fell into your bed, you mean."

I grinned. "He did that." I glanced at the time. "I best get going."

"Okay. I want more details at some point though." Her smile was wide and infectious, so it was impossible to keep my smirk at bay when I left the room, throwing her a quick wink as I went.

Making my way to collect my next appointment, I touched my iPad with the schedule details on and tried not to wince. "Mrs. Trent?" I looked around the waiting room and spotted the gray-haired woman with a cage on her lap. I kept the grin fixed on my face as she glanced over, while I surreptitiously eyeballed the carrycase latch.

Leading Mrs. Trent to the consultation room, I prepared myself for dealing with her demon cat. The irony of Mr. Snuggles's name was not lost on me. "So," I asked as she placed the cage on the metal table and I closed the door, "how may I help you today?"

"Well, Doctor Falon," she started as she unlocked the cage, and I did everything in my power to remain rooted to the spot and not take a step back, "Mr. Snuggles has an eye full of pus." I kept my face neutral while she continued. "It came on last night, and I really can't handle my baby being so uncomfortable." I nodded in what I hoped was perceived as sympathy and not "get your crazy-ass cat out of here."

"I see." I offered her a tentative quirk of my lips. "Can you place him on the table and hold him firmly for me?" It seemed I was going in, and within easy biting distance.

I edged toward the table once Mrs. Trent had Snuggles in her grip. At my movement, the cat turned his sharp gaze on me. I was certain the animal mocked me, looking innocent until I was close enough he'd be able to claw me.

Taking his head between my palms, I released a breath when he didn't immediately try to bite my finger off. His eye was infected, so he would need some drops. "Okay." I stepped back. "A course of eyedrops should do the trick." I smiled, practically lightheaded at having gone through the quick exam unscathed. A first.

Patting her cat, Mrs. Trent nodded and offered me a sweet smile. "Thanks, Doctor."

I grinned and turned to get the drops. Unlocking one of the medicine cabinets where we stored standard supplies, I tapped the information into my iPad and hit Print. A moment later, the sticky label with instructions was secured and I was ready to usher Mrs. Trent and Snuggles out of there.

As I turned to hand the medication over, Mrs. Trent spoke. "Can you apply the first ones for me, please? You're so good with him."

My eyes widened in horror, and my fixed grin

was back, so tight my face muscles screamed at me. "Sure." The words spilled out unplanned as I reluctantly edged closer to the demon cat.

The next four minutes were epic-battle worthy. From the evil glint in Snuggles's eyes, it was as if he'd planned the whole thing.

By the time I ushered Mrs. Trent and her demonic pet out, I had a multitude of scratches on my hands, some releasing steady drips of blood, and I was sure I had a couple on my face too. Before I was able to inspect the damage, my iPad beeped. I looked down and saw a last-minute appointment had been added. I glanced at the time, relieved I should be able to fit this one in before Tanner returned for our lunch date. My stomach did an immediate flip in excitement, and my dick twinged. Not the best reaction considering I had to step out into the waiting room and collect my next patient.

Quickly washing my hands, wincing at the cuts, I dabbed a paper towel across my face. The white towel came away with small drops of crimson. I rolled my eyes, thinking that if Scott was going to continue to steal my clients, it could happily be Mr. Snuggles.

Straightening myself, relieved my sore hand had calmed my erection, I opened the folder for more information on my next appointment as I left the examining room.

Rex, apparently.

I scanned for more details as I walked. It was a new client, a Rhodesian Ridgeback, age approximately two years old. I glanced around the waiting room; Rex was easy to spot. He was damn pony size. I never got over the fact of how huge these dogs were, nor how soft they could be.

"Rex." My eyes then drifted to the owner, and I grinned.

Tanner stood, a wide grin spread across his face. "Hey."

I tilted my head, my gaze drifting between Rex and Tanner, my grin still wide. "Do you want to come through?" I indicated the corridor behind me and watched as he stood, patting the dog's head and offering him words of reassurance. My stomach flipped. He was so gorgeous.

Heading toward me, his smile became a smirk as he looked me up and down. His eyes lingered briefly on my face, focusing on my small scratches. I shrugged them off and beamed. It took all my willpower to lead him away rather than leaning in to kiss him. Clearing my throat, I led him to the examination room. "So," I started once he was in the room and I'd closed the door behind him, "who do we have here?"

Tanner was crouched down next to Rex. He planted a kiss on the dog's head and stroked him gently. "Meet Rex."

Strangely, the two made an adorable pair. I snorted at the thought, earning me a raised brow from Tanner. It seemed like a bizarre word choice for him. Sexy, rugged, those rolled easier off the tongue, but still—

I took a slow step toward Rex and Tanner. While Rex was neither growling nor cowering, the breed was known for their stubbornness and protectiveness. Since Tanner had never mentioned picking up a dog, I could only assume he'd been this morning and had then collected Rex. That being the case, the dog wouldn't have formed an attachment yet, but he was bound to be nervous.

"So, what's this guy's story?" I kneeled in front of them both and flicked my gaze at Rex and then Tanner. I didn't attempt to reach out to Rex, waiting instead for him to give me a good sniff and then approach me.

Tanner's eyes filled with excitement. "I got a call just as I was starting work on the drywall saying this guy had arrived and was in need of a home and ready to be collected." He scratched the dog's ear as he continued, "I've been on their list for months now, so had already been approved. He was literally brought in this morning, and since they had all of Rex's paperwork and background, they wanted to rehome him immediately."

Joy surrounded every word he spoke. It was impossible not to get caught up in his enthusiasm. I smiled, my focus fixed on him.

"The dog's owners just split. They're both leaving their area, a couple of towns over, and were due to drop Rex off with his new owners. It seemed the new owner they'd had in place had a change of heart. So here he is."

"And here he is indeed." Smiling, I immediately considered the positive ramifications of Tanner having a pet. It meant he was settled, right? With no immediate plans to uproot and leave town? I glanced at Rex as he stood and edged closer to me and gave a good sniff. Since his tail wasn't lowered between his legs, I assumed he was feeling calm and more comfortable in his strange environment. Rex then nudged my hand. I stroked behind his ear, happy I'd passed his inspection. "He's gorgeous," I said. "Were you wanting him checked over?"

Tanner nodded. "Yeah, please. His paperwork

says he's up-to-date with his shots and stuff." He pulled folded papers from his back pocket and handed them to me. Before I took them, his thumb caressed my hand. My eyes shot to his and I grinned, my skin flushing from the contact. I opened the paperwork, skimming the information as he continued, "I just wanted you to check him over and make sure everything is fine." My gaze lifted at his words. He shrugged, looking decidedly sheepish. "Fuck, I feel like a new dad or some crap. I'm all nervous and excited." He chuckled.

A little piece of me melted. Tanner had already proved over our weekend together he could do gentle and caring just as well as he could do rough and protective. But *this* Tanner, the man filled with nervous, excited energy, was a whole new ballgame. My heart flipped. I was already en route to falling hard for him, not unexpected considering all the time we'd spent together. But Christ, after he admitted his feelings, after witnessing his emotions for the unwanted Rex, I was unable to deny that I'd arrived at the destination of being hopelessly in love with the man.

Swallowing back my emotions, I took the time to get myself in check. After just one weekend of being more than friends was hardly the time to be declaring myself. My smile was genuine when I finally got myself under control. "I get it." I reached out and squeezed his hand. "This is wonderful. *Rex* is wonderful. You'll be a great team."

Tanner didn't try to contain his excitement. His eyes were bright, and a buzz of energy surrounded him. It was a look I could happily get used to. He tugged my hand gently. Not enough to make me take a step forward, but enough to extend my arm closer to his body. Then he turned my wrist and pressed his lips to my sensitive flesh.

"Thank you." While a smirk chased his words, his voice had lowered, and more serious eyes peered over at me.

I cleared my throat, tried to calm my fluttering heart, and pressed my lips together, a grin still tugging at them. "Okay"—I reluctantly pulled my arm away—"let's have a look, shall we?" I eyed Rex with a quirk of my lips. He eyed me right back as if trying to work me out. I could only imagine the extra scents and tension in the room after I'd all but swooned over Tanner's words. "You comfortable holding on to Rex?"

I glanced at Tanner, who nodded. "He seems to be already so comfortable with you. Impressive," I appraised.

Edging back in front of Rex, Tanner moved to Rex's head and gave calming murmurs of reassurance. While Rex had allowed me to give him an ear rub, it didn't mean we were yet friends, and I had no desire to be at the end of his growls.

"That's because he's a good boy, and I was also told about his weakness for salmon," Tanner admitted.

I contained my laughter, not wanting to startle Rex, and shook my head. "Salmon, really?" Brushing Rex's coat, I carried out a basic exam while Tanner responded.

"Yeah, not the cheap tinned stuff either." Laughter chased his words. "Typical, right? This dog's going to cripple me." He ruffled Rex's ears and placed a kiss on his head. I watched on in wonder as I continued my exam. Their bond seemed pretty immediate. I was so glad for Tanner. He'd mentioned wanting a dog a few weeks back, but I hadn't realized how much.

I wondered what had driven him to the decision in the first place. I loved dogs; they were my first choice for pet selection. For me, it was definitely the desire for companionship that drove my desire for a pet. Life could get lonely at times, especially in the town I'd decided to call home. Maybe it was the same for Tanner.

I stood and headed to my iPad and entered a few notes from my quick exam, and updated the details from the paperwork Tanner had handed me.

"All good?" he asked.

I turned and nodded. "Perfect." Grabbing a dog treat from the container on the counter, I offered it to Rex. "Sorry, buddy, it's not salmon, but it's all I've got." Tanner laughed, and I threw him a wink as Rex carefully took the treat from my hand.

"Thanks for fitting us in."

I grinned. "I had an opening, and I have to say, it's the best surprise of my day."

He quirked his brow. "Is that so?"

"Yep." I nodded and then looked at the time. It was lunch.

Tanner's gaze followed mine, landing on the clock. "Well let's see if I can up that 'best surprise' to a fucking incredible one, shall we?" His smirk was mischievous.

Both my brows shot up. His confidence and playfulness were so sexy.

"Let me settle the bill, and I'll wait for you outside for—"

"No need." I grinned. "Your money's no good

here." Instead of a smile, his mouth dipped, and he frowned. "What? What's wrong?"

Tanner took a step toward me, stopping so we were virtually toe to toe. I had to angle my head slightly to look into his eyes. "I don't need you to do that. I can pay."

"Let me do this." I reached out a tentative hand and brushed my thumb across his lips. It was unlike me to initiate contact, especially with the newness of our relationship, but heck, how could I be expected to be so close and not touch him?

Before I could pull away, he snagged my hand with his free one, the other holding Rex's lead. With his gaze fixed on mine, once more he brushed his lips against my wrist; this time a flick of his tongue chased the action. "Thank you." His voice was gruff and sounded like sex.

I bit my bottom lip, and I wasn't quite sure if it was to hold back the groan from his kiss and gesture or to stop myself from giggling like a schoolboy and thinking his voice was sex. *What does that even mean?*

Tanner's eyes widened; this time mirth played in them. He released my hand, placed his thumb on my lip, and tugged lightly to free it. "Something funny?"

Apparently my amusement hadn't been hidden. With a wide grin, I shook my head, but not before capturing his thumb carefully in my mouth and wrapping my tongue around it. The grin that had begun to form on his face dropped. His eyes turned hooded. "You've got two minutes to get your hot-as-fuck ass outside and in my truck."

Removing his finger, he threw me a heated look. "Come on, Rex." He stepped around me, leaving me hard and needy. *Hot damn, I best get my butt outside pronto.*

With an extra bounce in my step, I rushed through the clinic like a whirlwind, gathering what I needed before finding myself in the parking lot and before Tanner, who stood leaning against his truck.

CHAPTER THIRTEEN

TANNER

CARTER WAS DOING ALL SORTS OF THINGS TO NOT only my body, but fuck, my heart as well. He yanked out emotions I'd never experienced before. I loved my family, Davis and Libby, something fierce, and had loved my parents, even my unaccepting prick of a dad. They'd died several years back, only two years apart. Their loss was something I'd dealt with a good while ago. It didn't mean I didn't miss them. Instead, I put all my energy into what I had. That was Davis, which had then extended to Libby, and now included Carter.

I could admit to myself that no other guy had made me feel anywhere close to what I did for Carter. And wasn't that a mind and heart fuck.

It wasn't like I was anti-relationships. It was

just… unexpected. I hadn't been looking to meet anyone, but then he'd happened. Fell on his ass at my feet and showed me his cock. I laughed to myself. Yeah, there was no coming back from that.

My gaze remained on the clinic's entrance, waiting for Carter to exit for lunch. I wanted nothing more than to race home so I could bury myself in him. I craved the connection, the need to feel him wrapped around me. But the thirty minutes we had wouldn't allow any of that to happen.

I pulled my shades on top of my head when he stepped out of the building. Our eyes connected and almost simultaneously we grinned at each other. I was sure he had no idea how goddamn sexy he was. But that was okay. I would happily make it my mission to remind him every day.

"Hey," he called out in greeting as he stepped closer.

As soon as he was before me, I tugged him close and pressed a chaste kiss to his lips. Then I side-stepped and opened the passenger door for him.

"Wow, Mr. Grady, so chivalrous." He chuckled lightly. I took great pleasure in swatting his ass and making him grunt as he made to get in the cab. "Ouch." He rubbed his ass and tossed a look my way.

I grinned in response and made my way to the driver side.

"Thirty minutes, right?" I thought it best to confirm just in case I'd got it wrong and we could make a quick escape, but no such luck when he answered.

"Yep. And considering, well, everything... it's best that I'm not late."

My shoulders tensed at the reminder. With the manic day I'd had with Rex, Carter's loser boss had been pushed to the back of my mind. I tried to keep the grit out of my voice when I responded "Okay," but I wasn't sure how convincing I was since his hand appeared on my leg and he squeezed.

"It's all good." His calm voice had me glancing at him. "Seriously. I've actually had a great morning, topped off with your unexpected visit."

I nodded with a lift of my lips, put the truck in gear, and clasped my hand on his before heading out of the parking lot. Knowing his morning had been good with no added bullshit released some of my tension, but one good morning didn't mean the idiot would stop the bullying BS he'd been pulling on Carter. I was confident it would take more than a warning growl from me to do the trick, so I was still determined to find a way to support him. And if all else failed, kicking his ass was always an option.

Pulling over a few minutes later at the enclosed dog park, I scanned the area. Rex and I had a lot of bonding to do. Apparently he was good with other dogs, but who knew until I saw that for myself. Once parked, I pressed a kiss to Carter's hand before telling him, "Come on. Let's eat." We climbed out, and I collected the bag from the back seat and Rex from the rear trailer, unlocking his safety cage. Then I nodded toward one of the picnic benches.

It was late May, and summer hadn't properly kicked in yet, but it was just warm enough to sit outside comfortably and enjoy the sun and fresh air. We sat, Rex still on his lead and having a sniff around, and I pulled out the sandwiches I'd managed to throw together after collecting Rex. I also pulled out juice, apples, and some potato chips.

When I glanced up, I faltered. Carter's head was tilted slightly to the side, his eyes locked on my face. His bottom lip was captured by his teeth. I rose a little and leaned over to him. Once close, I pressed my mouth to his. Fuck, I didn't think I'd ever get enough of him.

I'd never been into PDA and while I had no plans to start a heavy make-out session with Carter,

sharing sweet kisses with him whenever I wanted...
yeah, I could happily get used to it.

After I pulled away and placed his food before
him, he pressed two fingers against his lips. "What
was that for?" I raised my brows in amusement.
"Don't get me wrong, I liked it and you can happily
do it whenever you want—"

"And wherever I want?" I asked, my words laced
with mischief.

He blushed and then nodded. "Yeah, I have no
problem with that."

"Good. So I don't need to explain myself, right?"

Wide-eyed, he looked back at me, and he
suddenly seemed uncertain.

I sighed lightly. "I like kissing you, touching you,
especially whenever and *wherever* I want. If I want to
and you're good with it, I will do exactly that.
Okay?"

He nodded again, and this time he smiled.

"Eat," I encouraged. "You don't have long."

I watched as he picked up the sandwich I'd made
for him and an unfamiliar longing twisted in my gut.
I'd never made a guy food before—Davis didn't
count—even a lousy sandwich. And from the way he
smirked with every bite and looked around our
surroundings with genuine happiness on his face, I

would make him lunch every day if this was his reaction.

It didn't take us long to finish eating. I stood, apple in hand, and indicated the enclosed area created specifically for dogs. "You coming?"

He bit into his own apple and bobbed his head. Once he swallowed, he said, "You go ahead. I'll tidy this, put the bag in your truck, and then join you."

"Thanks." I looked down at Rex, who waited patiently beside me. "You ready for a run, boy?" He tilted his head as if listening to me. Grinning, I said, "Come on then," and led him to the gate.

"What are your plans for today?" Carter asked once he joined me. I'd immediately taken his hand, which caused him to smile sweetly at me.

With my eyes still on Rex as he ran and sniffed around the empty run, I answered, "I'm going to continue in the spare room. Because I picked up Rex, I'm a bit behind."

His hand squeezed mine, and he nudged his shoulder against me. His voice was light and sounded amused when he said, "Hardly behind. Geez, you've been working your butt off doing above and beyond the hours needed. Anyone would think you were trying to get done as quickly as possible to get the heck out of there."

I knew he jested, but it didn't stop me from turning him toward me. "Is that what you think, huh?" I kept my tone light to match his, but there was also a part of me that wondered if there was maybe a slight edge of concern in his voice.

He shrugged and grinned in answer. "Not really." He scrunched his nose as if considering his words. "I'm sure you'd like some free time back though."

I nodded. "Damn straight I would." Before he had the chance to readjust his face into a frown, I knocked that nonsense on the head immediately. "It means I get uninterrupted time with you when I'm picking you up off the floor or having to get you hosed down after you've stepped in paint or something."

With twitching lips and a mock frown, he scolded, "I'm the best laborer you've ever had, and you know it."

I tugged him toward me so his body was flush against mine. Then, leaning down, I brushed my lips against his ear, licking and nibbling lightly before saying, "The fucking sexiest." I pulled away. Carter's eyes were closed, and pink touched his cheeks. "Plus, any chance I have to get you in a shower is a good thing."

He laughed loudly. Before he could speak, a bark

drew our attention. It wasn't Rex, although the arrival had gotten his attention.

Carter stepped out of my arms when the old lady approached, a yapping dog at her heels. I didn't allow Carter to get far before I snagged him by the waist and pulled him to my side. I was pretty sure we would soon become gossip fodder. Me, a relative nobody in town, making out with the new veterinarian. But that was all fine by me.

I'd never had the time or patience for gossips or assholes. And from all I'd learned about Carter, I knew he was open about who he was.

Carter's voice surprised me. "Hey, Mrs. Carlisle. How're things?" I looked down at him, trying to get a read on his expression. He was relaxed. His arm had moved to around my waist when I'd hauled him to me, and it remained in place.

Reassured, I then looked over at Mrs. Carlisle. She was a small woman, so I was surprised that I wanted to take a step back. Her gaze was hard. There was steel in her eyes, even her slightly wonky one. She stepped closer, cane tapping on the pavement with every step, her pet rat close to her side. I considered swooping Carter up and making a run for it. It was only his relaxed state that prevented me.

Once in front of us, her gaze landed on Carter.

Her smile came quickly. "How are you, Dr. Falon? It's lovely to see you out and about and not stuck in the clinic." She reached for her bag that hung over her arm, opened it and pulled out a bag. "Here, Doc. Have some lemon drops." She held them out to Carter, who reached forward and took them.

"Mrs. Carlisle, you know they're my favorite. You're so good to me."

She nodded, her eyes crinkling at the corners as he spoke. When he'd finished speaking, her gaze snapped to mine. I stood a little taller as she examined me, while her rogue eye put the fear of God in me as it roamed in a different direction.

"You, boy." I was tempted to look around. It had been a long time since I'd been referred to as a boy. "What are your intentions with our good doctor here?"

My mouth dropped open. She didn't even give me the chance to answer before she said, "Cat got your tongue? Speak up."

I cleared my throat. "Well, erm—" Carter's hand squeezed my waist tightly, and by the slight movement coming from him, his rocking against my tense body, I knew the cheeky fucker was laughing. That changed everything. There was no way I'd let this situation get the better of me. *Carter thinks it's funny?* "Actually, Mrs.… Carlisle?"

"Something wrong with your hearing? The good doc's used my name twice already."

Carter's vibrations at my side grew significantly. My fingers flexed at his side, before shifting to his ass. I squeezed, which immediately stopped his movement. The sound of his breath catching was perfect and urged me on. I grinned. "Mrs. Carlisle, I'm pleased you asked." Her brows lifted in expectation. "The *good doc* here and I were just about to head back to the clinic. But not before I took him to the local lookout"—I had no idea if there was such a place, but there usually was one in every town—"where I planned to make him all hot and sweaty by kissing him thoroughly, get that sexy blush covering his sweet cheeks, before letting him go on his merry way to work."

I was desperate to look at Carter, sure his mouth would be gaping and he'd be impersonating a fish. Instead, I offered Mrs. Carlisle the most innocent smile I could and waited.

She nodded, seemingly pleased. "Good. Now get that horny dog of yours away before I let Belinda in there for a run. All the damn dogs are after a piece of her tail." She turned to step away, then paused and looked back at us. "And make sure you use protection. You seem like a nice young man, if not a little wicked. Just make sure you wrap up."

Sure my eyes were going to pop out of my head, I stood frozen. How the fuck was I to respond to that? I couldn't, so instead, I remained silent.

"Bye, Mrs. Carlisle," Carter called as he released me and went to call Rex over.

I still stood there when Carter returned with Rex on his lead. Laughter lit his eyes.

"Who the fuck was that?"

He just laughed and shook his head. "Welcome to my world." He snorted. "Where every client has something to say about how you live your life." He took my hand and tugged. "Come on, you *wicked* man. You need to get me back to work so I'm not late."

CHAPTER FOURTEEN

CARTER

Tanner's progress on the house was impressive. Already parts of the house were transformed, and I could finally use the staircase without fearing for my life.

I held the newly replaced banister as I headed upstairs to grab a shower in my new en suite. Tanner had called someone in to replace and tile it, and it was finally finished. After just three days of its sparkling newness, I was nowhere near close to no longer being excited to use it, or simply step in and stare at it for a while. Admittedly, Tanner had already caught me having three showers in one day. Though two of those times had involved him joining me, so he didn't tease me so much about those.

I'd had a long and busy shift at work with an early start and a midnight emergency call out. I'd managed to come back home by about two before having to return for six. I thought I'd be too hyped and awake to sleep, but once I was in bed and Tanner wrapped his big body around me, before I knew it, he was waking me with a kiss on my nose and coffee in his hand.

Life and work, and definitely my love life were pretty awesome, and I hoped it stretched out indefinitely. There'd been no more work dramas since the confrontation between Scott and Tanner a few weeks back, which was a blessing, and things were progressing naturally with Tanner and me.

That night we were actually having dinner with Davis. I was looking forward to finally meeting him and Libby. I'd heard a lot about them already and knew how important they were to Tanner. But it was that knowledge that also made me nervous as heck.

I looked at the time and checked the oven, even knowing the chicken wouldn't be ready yet.

"You know, that's the third time you've checked in ten minutes." Tanner's heat pressed against my back as his arms wrapped around my waist. "There's nothing to be nervous about, you know that, right?" Gentle lips touched my neck, his stubble grazing my skin and successfully distracting me.

"Uh-huh," I managed, angling my head, granting him better access.

His soft chuckle brushed warm air across my skin, before his lips rested against me again. Immediately I sighed, and my tension eased a little. "It's just—" His lips traveled up my neck. "—Davis." Breath swept past my ear and I shuddered, loving the feel. When his mouth landed on my earlobe, I groaned and then gasped when he took it between his teeth and tugged gently.

My groan turned into one of frustration when he pulled away. But I needn't have worried. He turned me in his arms and then heaved me close. "You know, we have twenty minutes." Firm hands clamped on my butt and he pulled my groin to his. "I could distract you. Christ, I could make you so fucking boneless that by the time they get here, you won't give a flying fuck."

I swallowed hard and was so tempted to take him up on the offer. "Twenty minutes?" I raised my brow in question.

He nodded, a grin that looked far too smug and

sexy lifting his lips. Giving my ass a squeeze, he tilted his head in offer.

With a frustrated groan, I sighed, pecked his lips and then wrangled myself out of his arms. "There's no way I'm going to be a hot sweaty mess when Davis gets here. Especially since your niece is going to be here too." I shook my head in horror and then frowned at him, shooting him a disapproving look when he burst into laughter.

"You know Libby's not even crawling yet, right?" He snorted before heading to the fridge and removing a beer.

I twisted my lips at him and raised my brows, waiting for him to stop laughing.

"What?" He paused, beer bottle an inch from his lips.

"You finished?"

He looked confused for a moment, looked at his beer a second before he rolled his eyes at me. While his laughter had stopped, a smile still tilted his lips. "I know you're nervous." He stepped toward me, placed his bottle on the surface behind me, and threaded a finger through one of my belt loops. "And, it's… sweet that you're trying so hard and want to make a good impression." He tugged me to him, pressing his lips gently to mine before easing back slightly. "But, babe, honestly, Davis is my best friend, my brother, you know this, and with that, he's happy as long as I'm happy."

I swallowed, nerves bubbling in my chest. I cleared my throat. "Are you happy?" While I pretty much figured he was, since, well, everything was amazing, I needed to hear the words. I tried not to be needy and rarely made demands, but sometimes I genuinely needed to hear stuff like this. While our physical connection was intense and passionate— and I seriously had not experienced such magnificent sex with another man like I had with him— Tanner wasn't great at sharing his feelings. There was the occasional moment when he'd let his guard down for words to spill out. But they were rare.

On the flip side, I was sure he was honest when he showed me how he felt. Each touch, kiss, and caress, both in and out of the bedroom, meant something. I just wasn't sure what the "something" meant to him. And while we'd shared some bits from our past as well as looking to the future, we hadn't reached the point of sharing the big stuff. Yet. God, I was there already, on the edge of shouting to him, to the world that when he'd said that he needed me, wanted me that first time, I was his, and I loved him.

But standing in the kitchen waiting to meet

people he loved, my vulnerability rose to the surface as I waited for his answer. His eyes softened, and he dipped his head a little lower, tipping my chin up to ensure I made eye contact with him. "Yes."

And that was it.

No flowery words. No explanation. No big speech about the ways he was happy or even how *I* made him happy.

But that one word was enough. My smile stretched my mouth wide, and tension slipped from my body. His gaze roamed my face, and I wondered if he could see how that single syllable affected me, the ease it instilled in me.

I swallowed again, but this time it was to gain control of my emotions, keep in check my relief. My eyes landed on his lips when they curved. "We good?"

I nodded, not daring to speak in case my voice gave my emotions away. Nor did I want to break the spell of this moment.

With another quick glance at my eyes, as if he was making sure I was telling him the truth, he seemed satisfied. He bobbed his head once, gave me a quick kiss, then smacked my ass as he headed away from me.

"Where are you going?" I asked once I found my voice.

"He's here."

"Huh?" I sought out the time. Davis was early. "But how—?"

"Heard his car pull up outside."

Huh? My senses beyond that of watching and listening to Tanner had apparently switched off over the past five minutes or so. I glanced at the oven, tempted to recheck it, but instead, I forced my feet to move. It was time to meet Tanner's family.

———

I snorted, almost spilling the contents of my glass. "And then what did he do?" I threw a quick glance at Tanner and raised my brows when I saw heat creep across his cheeks. Obviously, whatever dirt Davis was about to dish was good.

"Don't you fucking dare," Tanner growled at Davis. The sound was gravelly and so husky I mentally stored the sound away to see if he'd use it in the bedroom one time. I dragged my gaze away from him, mildly aware I'd probably had too much wine since I was struggling to keep my mind focused on Davis's story and not Tanner and the bedroom.

"What?" Davis grinned, his eyes shining with glee. "You don't want Carter to know about having to call fire and rescue?"

Now I was intrigued. "Go on. You can't stop now," I encouraged. I determinedly kept my eyes off Tanner, sure he was giving me a hard stare.

Davis grinned, threw Tanner the finger and me a wink. "He clambered to the men's and tried scrambling out the window." I snorted, wide-eyed, trying to imagine Tanner ever running from anything. "Then," Davis continued, tears threatening to spill from his eyes in amusement, "the window was in one of the cubicles. He slipped and somehow got his foot wedged in the bowl."

Loud laughter erupted from me, and I clamped a hand over my mouth, risking a quick look at Tanner. Despite his frown and squinting eyes, there was no hardness reflected there. He rolled his eyes in mock irritation. "Yeah, yeah, lap it up. It was the heel that did it. It was strapped so tight to my fucking foot, I couldn't get the thing off. I still have no idea how it happened."

Davis kept laughing, the sound loud and contagious. "When...," he gasped. "When the firefighters arrived, it turned out that we knew one of the firemen. It didn't take long for the word to spread that

Tanner had been caught in fishnets and heels, trying to escape a gaggle of women."

I could see it now. The image was ridiculous. Tanner—tall, strong, just the right side of muscular Tanner—dressed up in drag, and then having to flee from horny old women. My face started to hurt from the laughter and my wide smile, but I needed to know. "Please tell me you have photographic evidence."

"Hey now." Tanner snaked his arm around my waist and dragged me to him, holding me close with no chance of escape. Not that I had any desire to be released. "No, there isn't." His voice was gruff but held amusement.

I looked at Davis for confirmation. He shrugged. "Unbelievably no. It's a fucking travesty really. I could have held it over his head on so many occasi —" A throw cushion landed in his face. "*Oomph.*"

Tanner chuckled and pressed a kiss to my neck. I sighed at the contact. "He didn't tell you that I was only in drag for a charity event."

"Oh," I said with a grin, "you don't make a habit of dressing up in women's clothes and wearing makeup?" I twisted my head to look at him, throwing him a wink.

He twisted his mouth as if deciding just how to

punish me for my ribbing. The look in his eyes had me swallowing in delight. Damn, just one look from this man and I was a needy mess.

"No," he finally answered.

Davis's snort brought our attention back to him. "It's true," he admitted. "And I will say, that group of women were fucking terrifying. I'd have run too."

Aware I was practically sitting on Tanner's lap, I wriggled against him and tapped his hand, intending for him to release me. Instead, a grunt of disapproval brushed across my ear. I bit my lip, embarrassment heating my cheeks since we had company.

"Don't mind me." I flicked my gaze to Davis in surprise. His smile was warm and genuine. "It's a nice change. Never seen my brother here all loved up." I held my breath at his words, and a moment later, Tanner's arm gripped me a little tighter and his fingers found the flesh of my side, and stroked small circles there. Davis sent Tanner a chin lift. "Looks good on you."

Having no idea how on earth I was meant to respond to that, I hesitated. Just as I opened my mouth to speak, still not quite sure what was going to fall out of my mouth, the soft gurgling of Libby dragged my attention to her.

I'd never been more relieved for a break in tension, though I was convinced I was the only idiot who felt it. Davis looked perfectly relaxed, while Tanner had made my insides mushy with his distracting touch.

I smiled over at Libby as she pulled her feet high and reached out and took them in her hands before she spotted Rex, who lay patiently by her side and was staring at her with interest. She'd been fast asleep for the past couple of hours and was lying on a collection of blankets on the floor while Rex had taken on the role of protector.

When she spotted Rex, she garbled noises and turned herself toward him. She lay on her front reaching out for him, seemingly desperate to get her legs moving in a crawling motion, but they didn't seem to be behaving.

Rex shuffled toward Libby and placed his head on the floor before her. She giggled in delight and reached out, her hand on his fur.

"Hey, baby girl." Warmth filled Davis's voice when he spoke to his daughter. He stood, walked over to her, and then reached down to swoop her into his arms. He patted Rex's head too, who seemed a little lost without Libby to lick. "You hungry?" A happy smile lit her face before it was hidden by her cramming a few of her fingers in her mouth.

I laughed. "Looks like it to me."

Davis faced me with a grin. "Mind if I use your kitchen to heat her food?"

"Of course not. I can do it if—"

"No need." He stepped over, passed Libby to me, released a loud snort-laugh at my startled face, and then left the room.

"All righty then." I looked down at Libby. She was so small that I had no clue how to even hold her without breaking her.

Tanner's soft chuckle had me quickly glancing over at him, my eyes wide in horror and pleading for help. He grinned, shifted me off him, and proceeded to get off the sofa and kneel before me. He pressed a kiss to my forehead and then one to Libby's. Immediately she cooed and wriggled, lifting her head.

"Tanner?" I seriously had no idea what to do. I'd never held a baby before. Pups, kittens, heck, even calves, those I could handle, but a human baby had small beads of sweat breaking out on the back of my neck.

"You're fine." His voice was calming, and I chose to ignore the humor in his tone. "Just let her stand up. She wants to look around and take everything in. Davis said she's trying her hardest to stand by herself. She's not there yet." He sounded amused.

"But—"

"She won't break."

Dammit, he already knew me so well.

"Really," he continued, "she's a sturdy little thing. She's already trying to crawl. To be honest, I'm surprised she isn't demanding to be set down so she can drag herself around."

I nodded, some of my stress dissipating. I knew she wasn't a newborn or anything, but I hadn't a clue about babies, or how to figure out how old they were, let alone what they could do at different stages. I stood Libby upright on my knees where she eyed me in what I hoped was interest and not wariness.

After a few moments of awkwardness and staring wide-eyed at each other, Libby flashed a gummy smile at me. A large grin plastered my face, and I cooed at her, feeling as though I'd achieved something monumental to get such a reaction from her.

"You see, nothing to worry about." Tanner's palm pressed against my arm, giving me a light squeeze.

Angling my head to look at him, I puffed my chest in pride.

"She likes me."

He laughed. "Seems that way."

"Awesome." Davis stepped back into the room carrying a bowl and a small plastic spoon. "I'll put you on the top of the list for babysitting."

I'd looked away from him when he'd entered, but his words made me jerk my head back to him in such a hurry, I was sure I'd pulled something. "What?"

Loud laughter burst from him. "You'll be fine." He winked.

With a frown, I nodded, having no clue if he was joking or not.

Davis picked up his daughter and returned to his chair, placing her on his knee. No sooner had he sat than Tanner stood, rummaged around in a huge bag sitting next to Davis, pulled a bib free, and put it on Libby. He planted a quick kiss on her head before grabbing a baby bottle from the bag too. He disappeared for a moment as Davis started feeding Libby tiny mouthfuls of a mushed-up orange substance that made her hum in appreciation.

A moment later Tanner was back, the bottle filled

with water. He placed it next to Davis so it was in easy reach.

I'd watched the whole exchange in wide-eyed silence. "Wow." The word tumbled from my lips. Both men looked at me and heat touched my cheeks. I hadn't intended to say anything.

"What's that?" Tanner tilted his head in question.

"Just, you guys are so in sync with each other. You don't even have to speak to get the job done and look after her." A pang of jealousy threatened to bloom in my chest, but I pushed it aside. Instead, I grasped on to the other emotion that had risen: pride.

I saw the concern in Tanner's eyes as he looked at me. Needing to eliminate that reaction, I smiled, pushing as much warmth and reassurance as possible into it as I could. "It's impressive, that's all."

When my gaze flicked to Davis, I realized he'd watched the whole exchange. I kept my smile in place. While it was genuine, his focus sent a pulse of nerves through me. "So," I continued, once again with no real clue as to what to say, but my hate of awkward silence spurred me on, "are you looking for a baby-mama for Libby?"

Immediately I wanted to smack myself upside the head and then race out of the room to run and hide.

What on earth was I doing, saying? *Baby-mama?* I wanted to gag a little that such words had come out of my mouth. I blamed a couple of the nurses from work who watched crap TV. I must've walked into a dodgy conversation and that horrendous description quite possibly cemented itself in my brain unbidden.

My eyes grew wide in horror. I risked a glance at Tanner, hoping he wasn't annoyed at me, and desperately praying he'd be there to help yank my foot out of my mouth.

Well, he wasn't mad.

He seemed concerned for my mental health if the confusion painted on his face was anything to go by, but he was also holding back laughter. His lips twitched, and his eyes were bright with amusement. I cast my gaze at Davis. Both horror and relief swirled; his expression and reaction were similar to Tanner's. But I was mortified. *Way to make an impression!*

"I, er, please don't answer that." I seriously had nothing. There was no comeback to the nonsense I'd spouted. I looked at the door, seeing a possible escape route. "Another drink?" I all but leaped out of my seat. Davis's eyes grew even wider. I hesitated for a moment, knowing I had to wait for a response, but desperate to get out of the room and throw myself in the freezer to cool my flaming cheeks.

An amused grin spread across Davis's face. Laughing, he said, "It's all good. Seriously. Sit your ass down. I'm all right." He shoveled another spoonful of food into Libby's mouth and then returned his attention to me.

I hovered, unsure what to do.

"Carter."

I met Tanner's gaze.

"Come and sit." He patted the space next to him.

I released a heavy sigh, trying my hardest to swallow my embarrassment and act unaffected. "Okay." I nodded, and threw him a strained smile. When my butt hit the cushion next to him, Tanner wrapped his arm around me, and he hugged me closer to his side.

"You okay?"

"Yeah, sure." I glanced at Tanner, who quirked his lips. "You know how my mouth gets the better of me sometimes." Admittedly it didn't do that often, but I was grasping at straws. "Sorry," I said on an exhale. "That was really inappropriate." I looked at Davis as I spoke. He just grinned back, still amused.

I knew the bare bones of Davis's history. That he grew up with Tanner, and they were as close as brothers. I also knew that Libby was the product of a one-night stand and that her mom had split. It was still bizarre to me that the split was willing, with Davis taking on full custody. But heck, men skipped out on women all the time I supposed, so why should it be any different for a woman?

"Seriously, it's fine. There's nothing wrong with the question." Davis paused. "Okay, baby-mama may have thrown me a little." He laughed, which in turn made Libby giggle too. Davis dropped a kiss to her head before he spooned more food into her mouth and said, "And to answer your question, no. Libby and I are pretty cool as we are. I have no idea how I'd even fit in a relationship on top of work and Libby.

"Maybe one day I'll meet the right person, but I'm in no rush." Libby made a strange noise, and I watched her start to shake her head. Davis moved her a little, placing the bowl and spoon on the floor, which Rex immediately attacked, ignoring Tanner's grumbles and much to Libby's delight. Davis then picked up the water bottle and handed it to Libby, who latched on to it with both hands. Then he looked at me with a wide smile. "And who said it would have to be a mama anyway?" He waggled his eyebrows up and down.

Tanner snorted beside me and I felt movement. He was chuckling and shaking his head.

"Oh." I nodded, admittedly thrown. I'd assumed Davis was straight since he was a dad, especially since I knew the brief history of Libby's conception. "Well." I shrugged like a doofus, tilted my head, and laughed. "At least that way you have more options."

CHAPTER FIFTEEN

TANNER

"He's good for you."

"That's one heck of a greeting." I raised my brows at Davis, kissed Libby on the cheek and then handed her to him. It was the first chance I'd had to see Davis since he'd been by Carter's a few days earlier. I'd picked Libby up from childcare and spent a couple of hours looking after her.

"Hey, baby girl." Davis covered his daughter's face with kisses, making her giggle. "Beer?" He looked at me before turning and heading to the kitchen.

"Yeah, thanks." I closed the door and followed him in, placing Libby's diaper bag on the floor at the bottom of the staircase.

When I entered the kitchen, Davis was strapping Libby into her high chair. After ensuring she was secure, he headed to the refrigerator and pulled out a couple of beers. He handed me one. "She all good?"

"Yep. They've written in her daily form a few notes for you. I had a quick glance, but I don't think there's anything life changing on there." It was hard to believe how both our lives had changed. God, a year ago, I would never have thought for one fucking second I'd have a conversation, with Davis of all people, about childcare notes, let alone know what I was talking about when it came to teething, colic, or diaper rash.

But shit, there we were, two jerk offs doting on a baby girl who managed to have us under her little finger without even being able to speak yet.

"Thanks." He took a gulp of beer as he moved around the kitchen to prepare dinner. "So yeah," he threw over his shoulder, "he is good for you. I like him."

I grinned. How could I not? As much as Davis and I had been dickwads over the years, his opinion mattered. Not that I'd be splitting with Carter if Davis thought he was a douche, but that he liked him made everything a whole lot easier.

"I like him too," I admitted.

Davis paused in preparing dinner to look at me. "Well fuck me silly!"

I snorted. "What?"

"You."

I lifted my brow, needing more to go on.

"In all these years not once have you admitted to liking a guy." When I rolled my eyes, he squinted and pointed his finger at me. With a snort, he said, "Seriously, you fucker, I know you wanted me to meet him, and yeah, that told me this guy was important, but you *like* him like him."

I shook my head. "You going to start trying to braid my fucking hair or something? Damn, Davis, what is this, middle school?"

"Screw you, asswipe." He grinned at me before turning on the stove. "I'm happy for you. You balance each other out or some BS like that," he said with a shrug. "I'm glad you're happy."

I really was. At one time, I would have thought admitting those sorts of feelings would have made me feel like an idiot, but there was no panic, no desire to reevaluate my feelings. Instead, I was sure that Carter was the fucking one. And wasn't that a mindfuck? I grinned again, a response I was finding more commonplace over the past couple of months. "Thanks. I was thinking about asking him away for a weekend. Will you have Rex if I get it sorted?"

It was my brainwave earlier today. While we

spent virtually all our free time together, we tended to spend too many extra hours working on his renovations. It meant little time to take a break. While he'd spent some nights at my place, it was often easier to be at his—because of the work on his property.

The progress was great. I'd achieved a lot, and while there was still a way to go, the house finally felt safe, as in I no longer feared for my life when working in the place, wondering if a wall would collapse or a floor would give way.

Also, Carter hadn't said much at all about the bullying nonsense at work for a while. I'd asked him several times and he'd reassured me that apart from a few shitty glances thrown his way, nothing else had happened.

I believed him, based on the fact he didn't seem to be stressed about heading into work as much, but still, it had been a rough few weeks for him, so what better way to relax than getting away from it all?

"'Course I will," Davis answered. "You doing the whole romance thing... Christ, brother, I never thought I'd see the day." He laughed far too loudly.

"Whatever." Not the greatest comeback, but he did have a point. I'd been around the block a few times and wasn't renowned for commitment or romance, so we both knew this was a big deal. But Carter was worth it.

"Where you heading to?"

I sat down next to Libby and picked up one of the toys off her tray. I walked the weird dinosaur, doll monstrosity in front of her. She giggled in delight before she swiped it out of my hands. I carried on playing with her as I spoke. "I'm not sure. There's either the lakes or the city." They were such different places, offering various ways to fill our time. "What do you think?" Davis was worse than I was when it came to relationships, but still, I trusted him in most things.

"Depends." He stirred the pot as he continued, "You want idyllic romance before you fuck or drunken hard-core sex after partying?"

He was deadly serious. He was also right. I snorted at the both of us. "Should I want the first even though I'm really wanting the second?" Carter and I had never had drunken sex, so the idea had merits. Though a weekend of nothing but relaxing at the lakes did sound like something we could both do with. Plus, we wouldn't have to socialize or anything. God, I was getting old when I wasn't even bothering to debate the possibilities.

"Ha! If you take a couple of cases of beer with

you, then you could make some of the second choice happen." He threw me a wicked grin and took the food off the stove.

"Good point," I admitted. Just the thought of a weekend away, free from disturbances from real life sounded amazing. I pulled out my phone from my pocket and opened Google.

———

I HAD SOME INCREDIBLE STEALTH SKILLS. YEAH, I WAS a badass and decided that if construction went sideways, I had the makings of a spy. I snorted at the thought as I placed the bags in the back of my truck.

Earlier in the day, I'd dropped Rex off at Davis's and texted Lauren to ensure everything was set. When I'd first decided on this grand-gesture thing, it had seemed easy, but somehow it had spiraled into getting people I'd never even spoken to on board and me purchasing a couple of bottles of champagne.

I shook my head as I made sure the box of food, the bottles, and the crate of beer were all secure. Fucking champagne. When I'd stolen Carter's phone to grab Lauren's number—the only person who he'd really spoken about and was friendly with at work—

she'd agreed to ensure he wasn't on call and had then sent me on a mission with a list to make sure the weekend was apparently as romantic as fuck.

Hell, it wasn't like I was proposing to the guy. Yet. The thought made me grin. I'd tagged on that word a few times over the past few weeks, recognizing that the thought didn't make me freak out. We weren't near that stage. Christ, it could be another year or two for all I knew, but I saw Carter in my future. With all that driving me forward, I'd relented and paid a crazy amount of money for a couple of bottles of champagne. I was now off to pick up Carter.

Since it was Friday, he finished at two. The plan was to pick him up and sweep him away. The drive to the lakes was just a couple of hours, giving us plenty of time to settle in for the weekend. It was the peak of summer, with the weather fine, if not a little hot at times. The cabin we were staying at had air-conditioning, a row boat, and sat on a lake.

I was eager to start our weekend of escape.

Carter greeted me with warmth. He was expecting me, since I'd dropped him off for his shift so he was without his car. Lauren exited with him.

"Have a great weekend," she called, and waved.

"Thanks," Carter said as he stepped closer to me

and dropped a sweet kiss on my mouth. He pulled back and I stepped away to open the door for him.

"Thanks, Lauren." I threw her a chin lift and a wink, earning me a confused double take from Carter and a laugh from Lauren.

Before Carter could question me, I ushered him into the front seat and then made my way to the driver side. Before long, the engine was running and we were pulling out of the clinic's lot.

"Lauren?"

I grinned and threw him a quick wink. "Yeah, she seems great." From the corner of my eye, I saw him shift in his seat and angle himself slightly toward me.

"She is, but I'm wondering how you know that."

I gave a carefree one-shoulder shrug and a noncommittal grunt. I was sure he was squinting at me, no doubt a small frown forming between his brows, trying to figure things out. I kept my eyes firmly on the road though, wondering when he'd notice we were heading in the opposite direction of home.

"Music?" I asked as a way of distracting him.

It didn't work. No sooner had I said the word than his body shifted in his seat. I risked a glance at him and watched as he looked around.

"Erm, Tanner, not that I'm questioning your

awesome driving skills or anything, but you know this isn't the way home, right?"

I grinned and answered with a self-satisfied, "Yep," while I kept my eyes on the road, determined not to look at him in fear I'd break and tell him where we were heading. Somewhere between my random idea of heading away, to planning the break that had seemed to spiral a little out of control, to me driving the two of us to the cabin as a surprise, honest-to-God excitement had taken hold. It felt so fucking good to be doing something nice for Carter, and I couldn't wait till we arrived and I could see the reaction on his face.

I'd never done shit like this for anyone. Admittedly, there was no real long-term ex in my past, but still, the idea of pleasing him, being the reason to put a huge smile on his face, yeah, that did something to me.

"Yep?" His tone was amused, which I took as a win. At least he wasn't freaking out or something.

"Yep." I nodded. "Why don't you just sit back and relax. It'll take us a couple of hours."

From the slight movement of his body, I saw he was angled toward me again. "Okay." He reached out, placed a hand on my thigh, and gave it a light squeeze. My heart thudded in my chest at the contact as well as his trust. My hand quickly found his and we continued the journey drifting between companionable silence, and chatting about his day and the renovations.

———

"Hey, baby." I stroked Carter's cheek, waking him from his nap. He'd closed his eyes just twenty minutes or so earlier. I'd already grabbed the keys to the cabin and had even managed to unload the truck while he'd slept peacefully.

When Carter opened his eyes, his gaze quickly found mine. His expression tender, he stretched and pressed his cheek into my hand. "Hey."

"Come on." I stepped back out of the open car doorway.

Undoing his seat belt, he looked around, his eyes no doubt taking in the lake before landing on the cabin and then me. He climbed out and was immediately in my space, his body close to mine, so close he had to tilt his head to look into my eyes. "Something you need to tell me?" His voice was soft, almost a whisper.

My grin turned into a gentle quirk of my mouth as I cupped his face and pressed a quick, light kiss on his lips. "Surprise." I ended the word with a shrug and a half grin. I was sure he'd be excited, but still, my heart beat faster, pounding harder in my chest as I waited for his reaction.

His smile was addictive. It was the best damn look I'd ever seen on his face before. Warmth spread across his cheeks, the sort that wasn't embarrassment but happiness. I had no idea how I even knew it, but that look right there, the one he gave me... heck, my heart stuttered for a moment before restarting with a needy, demanding pound.

"You—" He cleared his throat. "You did this for me?"

It was on the tip of my tongue to be a wiseass and crack a joke; instead, I leaned down, brushed my lips to his, and answered, "Yeah, baby, it's all for you."

Apparently it was the right fucking thing to say, as I'd never seen Carter react so fast. In the barest of seconds, his sweet ass had climbed me like a tree. I stumbled as I adjusted to having his whole tight body wrapped around me. His mouth was on mine in a fierce and bruising kiss. My mouth angled to his as I welcomed the delicious assault of his tongue, his lips, and red-hot groans as he ground himself against me.

I gripped his ass to keep him from falling and to

hold him closer to me, loving every moment of friction, and everything he threw at me, but I needed to get him into the cabin before I took him in public.

I slowed the kiss down, despite his disgruntled moan, then pulled back, stopping the kiss. My gaze roamed his face, taking in the lust filling his eyes, and focused on his lips. Already they were a little swollen. Pressing my mouth to his neck, I inhaled the scent that was uniquely his. "Let's take this inside," I mumbled against his neck.

He nodded in approval. "Do you need me—"

I tightened my grip on his ass and spun around before taking purposeful strides to the cabin door. Thank Christ, I'd left the thing open.

"I'll take that as a no then." Amusement lifted his voice and he leaned in, resting his head on my shoulder, his face turned toward my neck so his warm breath hit my skin. His breathing was erratic, fast and irregular, pretty much mirroring my own.

Once inside, I pushed the door closed with my foot, and then took a step to the couch. I paused when Carter shook his head. "Bed?" I asked.

"Shower," he whispered.

Shower it was.

We made it to the en suite already buck naked and impressively injury free. No easy feat since the journey had taken us a good ten minutes of stumbling into walls, tripping over jeans, and me finding the willpower to wrench Carter's mouth off my erection.

We washed each other thoroughly, then I pressed Carter against the shower wall, still covered in soap suds, my mouth connected to his as our tongues swept against each other's. He hissed when I gripped him and stroked lazily. I wanted to take this slow, despite throbbing with the need to be deep inside him.

Hot, smooth, and wet, he was perfect in my palm. With a quick sweep of my thumb over his tip, his hiss turned into a groan. I swallowed the sound at the same time as my fingers traveled to his balls. I cupped them, giving him a gentle squeeze, then brushed back toward his ass, sweeping my finger against his puckered hole. Carter wrenched his mouth from mine.

"Fuck me, Tanner."

I laughed, my heart filling with emotion. Grinning, I leaned in and said against his neck, "You know I love it when you lose control enough to swear, baby." My lips against his flesh, I pressed against him once more before I pushed my finger into him. "Say it again."

This man of mine had the sweetest of mouths. Not only did he taste delicious and gave me the best head of my life, but the only time he ever swore was when he was seriously pissed off, or so needy for me that he couldn't keep his words straight. Pushing him to the edge and making his dirty mouth come to life was one of my favorite things. This time, he didn't disappoint.

"Tanner. Fuck. I need you."

I licked a path from his ear to his collarbone, then kissed and nipped my way to his chest. "What do you need?"

A gasp-groan escaped him and drew my gaze to his face. His neck was angled back, and his eyes were shut, his top teeth bit down on his bottom lip. I pressed my finger deeper inside him, watching his face closely. His eyes snapped open, and he peered down at me. Dragging my finger out slowly, I lowered to my knees with my gaze locked on his.

"What do you need?" I repeated.

"Everything." He groaned when I rewarded him by pushing back inside him and rubbed my chin against his bobbing shaft. "Just fuck me so fucking hard that I... I..." My tongue on his crown was a distraction, sure, but two uses of fuck in a sentence deserved a reward. "...I only feel you, only want you.

I want your tongue…" He gasped when said tongue wrapped around his head before lapping lightly at his slit. "…I want your tongue, your fingers, your cock, I want them everywhere." Carter's breath came out in heavy pants by the time he stopped speaking, and mine wasn't much better.

His words spurred me on. I wanted everything he said too. I wanted to bury myself inside him so deeply that he'd feel me when he dreamed, when he bathed, when he fucking brushed his goddamn teeth. I wanted to be the only one who would ever touch him again. Fuck it. I would be the only lucky bastard who would lay hands on him. There was no other possibility and no other explanation other than I loved this man with my whole heart and fucking soul.

Fuck.

I sprang up, taking both hands with me, and held his face between my palms. Two bright brown eyes peered back at me in surprise. My mouth slammed against his as I poured every ounce of feeling I had for this man into that one kiss, needing him to understand I was there. I wanted it all too.

"I love you," I finally said as I eased back from his mouth, my heart beating fiercely against my chest as my eyes met his.

The surprise had gone, lost in the heavy kiss we'd shared. But on my words, his eyes once more widened before softening, a smile lifting his cheeks. "I love you, too."

No hesitation. No stumble. Just four perfect words that undid me.

I grinned, my lips connecting with his briefly before I demanded, "Turn around, baby, let me show you how fucking much I love you."

His eyes all but rolled back in his head at my tone and instruction. Carter turned for me, his palms pressing against the shower wall. Short, heavy breaths mingled with the sound of the water splashing against our bodies and the floor.

After redirecting the spray a little so I wouldn't end up drowning, I sank to my knees and looked up. "Baby." He angled his head to look down at me. "This ass is mine." Even in the steam of the shower I watched in satisfaction as the heat of a blush rose on his cheeks.

I bit his ass lightly, causing a needy gasp from Carter. Then I opened him to me. Without me asking, he readjusted his feet and legs and bent just enough to give me access. Fuck me. His puckered hole was perfect.

I'd had too many fantasies of tasting him in the

best of ways, knowing above all else, my tongue would make him so goddamn hard, he'd be likely to come before I'd gotten my real fill of him. Leaning closer, I pressed my tongue gently against his opening, earning me an immediate groan of bliss. I lapped at him, all the time focusing on his response, wanting to know what would push him over the edge and give him the greatest pleasure.

Sex with Carter was easily the best I'd ever had. He was giving and eager to try new things as well as voicing his desire to satisfy me. That and knowing he loved me…. I eased my tongue into his channel, keeping the muscle stiff. God, I wanted this, wanted him, needed him every way I could get him.

Tight and perfect, he welcomed me into his body as he groaned and whimpered, sporadic "fucks" easing past his lips. When I pressed a hand against his lower back, encouraging him to bend even lower, he did so immediately. We moaned in unison as I penetrated deeper and felt him pulse around me.

"Fuck, I'm going to—"

Ripping my tongue from his body, I spun him around and latched on to his erection, taking him deep and sucking with everything I had. I hollowed my cheeks and sucked hard, grasping his ass to pull him even closer. The first hit of his cum against my tongue was in unison with Carter's words "Fuck, I love you." It was garbled and high-pitched, and I would have grinned if I wasn't busy pulling every drop out of him.

I eased off when he sagged against the wall, his fingertips brushing my hair and trailing against my cheek. Looking up at him, blinking past the splash of the water, my face brightened. He beamed back and indicated for me to stand. On my feet, I leaned against him, pressing a small kiss against his closed lips.

"Tired?"

He nodded.

"Come on then. Let's get you to bed."

Carter lifted a brow and then glanced between our bodies. I throbbed, but I wanted Carter rested and happy. I snorted at myself. Loved up and not looking out for my own poor cock.

"What?" he asked, amusement in the lilt of his voice.

"Nothing. But I can wait."

He didn't look convinced.

"I can," I answered with a small laugh. Admittedly, it was going to be hard to ignore, not only because of the fact I was rock-solid and was standing to attention, but it was always like this with Carter. I always wanted him. But at that moment, having gotten him off from sharing my tongue with him, that was fucking satisfying in itself. My impatient dick would have to wait.

I'd woken with Carter lowering himself on me. It was officially the best morning ever. Getting head in the morning was fucking incredible, but waking to him sheathing me inside my favorite place ever, yeah, hands down it was the best way to start the day. That and bareback, which we'd only recently been cleared for, had been fucking magic.

I'd come hard and fast. Not surprising since I'd fallen asleep with blue balls. But it was all worth it to start the day deep inside him. We'd since had breakfast and were walking around the lake, hand in hand, the epitome of a loving couple. Every time I thought it, I smirked like some sort of, well, enamored fool. Go figure.

We'd talked about the most random of shit, while also touching on our pasts too. Carter told me his parents would be heading into town in a month, which I was kinda anxious about. I'd never met a boyfriend's parents before, as ridiculous as it sounded. It was sort of pathetic I supposed, a guy in his thirties with no real committed relationships to speak of, but Carter thought it was sweet.

I rolled my eyes at him as he continued. "I think you were just saving yourself for me. Why go through the hassle of parents when they weren't mine?"

I laughed. "Yeah. That's exactly it."

"Shh, let me have my moment." Seriously, he was loving my virgin meeting-parents status a little too much. "But I suppose it was also so you wouldn't be scared off."

I snorted this time and tugged him to my side and placed a kiss on his temple. "Is that right?"

"Well." He looped his arm around my waist, and I wrapped my arm around his shoulder as we carried on walking. "My folks do come with a hazard label."

Over the past few weeks, Carter had shared a few stories about his mom and dad; most were hilarious, so I knew what he was getting at. "It'll be fine." As long as they liked me, of course. I'd lost my own parents when I was a teenager. I'd loved them and we'd had an okay relationship, but it had been a helluva long time since I'd been around parents who were acting in that role, if that made sense.

I knew they loved Carter, so despite my nerves, I

was confident that when they saw him happy, they'd like me. I'd make it so.

"Seriously, Tanner. You already know my mom has no filter, but when it comes to me and a relationship, she's going to lose her mind."

I paused and looked at him. "Have you not told her about us?"

He looked sheepish, and my heart would have dropped if he hadn't immediately pressed his lips to mine and whispered, "They're both going to love you, like *love* you, love you. But no, I haven't truthfully told her how serious we are." He took my hand and placed a kiss on my palm. "The only reason why is that as soon as she knows, she'll start buying *Rainbow Weddings* or something else as crazy."

I snorted and raised my brows. "Is there really a magazine call—"

He shrugged. "No idea. But the thing is, if there was, she'd buy it, and then start knitting—"

"Knitting?"

"Yes!" he said in earnest, color touching his cheeks and what looked like genuine fear making his eyes wide. He was fucking adorable. "Knitting for grandbabies."

I didn't even twitch, didn't move a muscle as I allowed that to settle in. Babies. I already knew I was the best uncle there was. I'd dealt with vomit, crap, piss, and so many tears and sleepless nights that the thought didn't terrify me. My breath caught at the possibility that at some point in the future Carter and I could have a kid of our own. I could see it, and wasn't that a fucking shock to my system?

"Oh shit." Carter swore, so whatever he saw in my reaction must have been bad. "Do you need to sit down? Oh Christ on a cracker, it's okay. I'll put them off from visiting. It's all talk anyway. You don't need to w—"

His words stopped when I shook my head. I met his gaze and swallowed, not quite sure how to even describe what was going on with me, let alone voice it. "Don't put them off."

"But—"

"I want to meet them. I can handle it." He didn't look quite convinced as he stood there, almost looking as if he were ready to catch me. "We can handle them together."

"Okay." He nodded, hesitation pouring from him.

"Yep." I finally smiled. "If your mom gets excited, that's great. It means she approves."

Carter's features softened. "Tanner, of course she'll approve. So will my dad. I love you." I didn't think hearing that would ever get old. "My loving you will be all they need to win them over."

I tugged him into my arms and before I kissed him, whispered, "Make sure she chooses pink wool."

His gasp was everything I hoped it would be. I loved taking Carter by surprise. As our lips locked and mouths moved against each other's, a small dip of his tongue seductively brushed against mine. He pulled up for air before I was ready, eliciting a disgruntled groan from me.

A giant grin spread across his lips. "Thank you."

"For what?" I asked.

"For not passing out."

I laughed loudly.

"I'm serious," he continued. "For a minute there, I thought you were a goner. Fortunately for you, I'm a doctor." He looked entirely too smug.

"Is that right?"

"Well, you're something akin to a gorilla at tim—"

The air whooshed out of him as I tackled him to the ground, turning as we landed so he fell on me. "Gorilla, huh?" I started laughing again, his shocked expression comical.

"Yes, definitely. What the heck was that?"

I shrugged and reached up to stroke his cheek.

"Didn't realize I needed an excuse to get you on top." I wriggled my brows at him.

Carter tutted, rolling his eyes at me. "True I suppose."

I leaned up and caught his lips with mine, before settling back down. "And for the record, I wasn't *that* freaked out."

A laugh-snort burst free from him. "You keep telling yourself that, buddy." He shifted, nudging against my growing erection, and I groaned at the contact. Concern lit his eyes at the sound. "You okay?"

I shook my head. I tilted my hips up and rubbed against him.

He arched one brow, his lips lifting. "You need me to kiss that better?"

I bit my cheeks to stop from grinning and nodded, wearing the most solemn face I could manage. "I think it's the only way to make this right and enable me to walk out of this alive."

Carter nibbled his bottom lip, his eyes hooding as he eased his way down my body and prepared to show me just how lifesaving his mouth could be.

CHAPTER SIXTEEN

CARTER

WE WATCHED FROM THE FRONT DOOR, MY HAND IN Tanner's, as my dad parked his car. I took a deep breath. "You ready for this?" Tanner squeezed my hand and released a small chuckle. I knew he wasn't taking this visit seriously. Yes, we'd had that "sort of" discussion a month ago at the lake, in addition to a few others since, plus I'd recounted my mom's loud squeal that had caused a ringing in my ears just two days earlier, but Tanner had no clue whatsoever what was going to hit him.

Two days. I had waited until the last possible moment to tell my parents Tanner and I were an item. I'd hoped a couple of days wouldn't be enough time for her to overprepare for their visit, or make any possible calls to my extended family. I knew there was a good chance my great-aunt in Scotland could have already heard and was starting to look at flights to the US. I wouldn't put it past my overexuberant mother.

When I'd admitted to my parents that Tanner, the same guy who'd worked his magic on my house over the past few months, was actually my boyfriend, my mom's squeal of "I knew it!" had set dogs howling everywhere within a three-mile radius. I was sure of it.

"She'll love me," Tanner reassured with a smirk as I looked at him.

"It's not that I'm worried about," I deadpanned. He winked and squeezed my hand once more. Just as I intended to plant a chaste kiss on his perfect lips, it began.

"Oh my goodness, Jack, will you look at that." I closed my eyes briefly, hoping to God that my mom wouldn't completely terrify Tanner. "Aren't they just adorable together?" And then, in a whirl of pink and perfume, she all but threw her handbag at Dad, who stood there open-armed in a well-rehearsed move, and she raced toward us.

A grin split my face as I wrapped her up in my arms. As much as my mom was certifiable at times, she was mine and awesome. "Hey, Mom." I kissed her on the cheek while attempting to step out of her bone-crushing hug. For five-foot-nothing, she was strong and gave some of the best hugs.

Not letting me out of her grasp just yet, she held me tighter, giving an extra squeeze as she said, "God, baby boy, I've missed you so much." She finally edged back a little and reached up and cupped my face in her palms. After a moment of silence as her perceptive eyes studied me, she finally returned my grin. "You look so handsome"—I rolled my eyes —"and happy." My heart squeezed. I really was happy, and the man somewhere behind me was the reason.

With the thought of Tanner firmly in my mind, I nodded. There was no way I could hold back from my mom. She read me far too easily, which was something of a blessing and a curse. I stepped out of her arms and looked over my shoulder at Tanner, stretching my arm out to him. He took my hand immediately. Rightness settled in my chest, warmth spreading through me at the contact. "Mom, Dad"— he'd finally reached us, laden with bags—"meet Tanner."

Mom lunged at Tanner, wrapping him up in her arms. Half-amused and half-mortified, I continued, "This crazy woman is Marcy and this good-looking chap"—I winked at my dad and patted him on the shoulder, not daring to hug him while he was over-loaded—"is Jack."

"Hey, son, you good?" My dad's deep voice held amusement as he shook his head slightly and indicated toward Mom, who had since released a bewildered Tanner but was now arm in arm with him as she dragged him toward the house.

"Yeah, Dad. Thanks." I gave a small but happy sigh. "Come on, let me help with some of the luggage." I took a bag out of his hands. "How long are you staying again?" I laughed.

"I best not tell you there're another two in the trunk then, huh?" he answered. I groaned in response. With a laugh, he said, "Don't worry, it's just a week."

I grinned as we walked toward the front door. Despite my anxiety of my mom possibly pushing us all over the edge, it was so good to see my parents. It was funny though, with the whirl in my stomach and tightening in my chest, I knew that Tanner meeting my parents was the more official declaration of our relationship. And that feeling right there was pretty wonderful.

. . .

Tanner had finally been introduced properly to my dad and had since disappeared with him on a tour of the house as he showed Dad all the renovations. The progress Tanner had made was phenomenal. The upstairs was finally completed with two fully functioning bathrooms, three bedrooms not only decorated but with doors that closed, and a staircase that was no longer a deathtrap. We'd celebrated the night Tanner had finally finished the staircase with me bent over as he'd taken me from behind. It was by far the best of ways to celebrate.

My gaze drifted away from said staircase and landed back on my mom. It was not the wisest of ideas to get wicked thoughts of Tanner, especially with my mom keenly observing me.

Her grin was wide and filled with happiness. "He's just lovely, and so very handsome."

Heat touched my cheeks. "He really is."

"So, how long have you been in love with him?" Her gaze was firm, her brows high in expectation and a clear "don't tell me any nonsense" vibe coming from her.

"Well." I cleared my throat. "Erm…."

She sighed. "Are you embarrassed about something?" she challenged.

"No." My reply was quick. "It's just…." In all

honesty, my reaction was bizarre even to me. But I knew the truth behind my heated cheeks. "Mom," I admitted, "God, I love him so much. He's just perfect." Tenderness filled her features as I spoke. "Don't get me wrong, he can be a pain in the butt too, but he's so perfect for me. He balances me out, and gets me all wound up in knots, and I just don't know... he just... he's it." Tears sprung to my eyes as Mom lifted her hands to cover her mouth and her own tears trailed down her face.

I cleared my throat, blinking away my emotion, trying in earnest not to let my gushy tears spill over. "So yeah, not embarrassed, just in love." I swallowed past the lump in my throat.

Reaching out to cup my face, Mom let her eyes roam my features. "I'm so happy for you, baby, so so happy. If he's everything you say he is and makes you this content, then he most definitely is perfect for you." She pulled back, wiped her eyes, and then stood. "Okay, I want to meet my grandbaby."

I frowned in confusion. I had no idea what on earth she was talking about. "Erm... Mom—"

Her cutting glance made me slam my mouth shut. "Rex, Carter. Seriously. Rex, this dog I've been hearing so much about."

She was off her rocker. I snorted, aware I was in

danger of a clip around the ear. "Mom, you know that's Tanner's dog, right?"

"Semantics," she said. "Is he out the back?"

He was. With all the time Tanner spent here, which had become pretty close to 24/7 with the exception of regular visits to see Davis and Libby, we'd made sure my yard was secured so that Rex could be at the house while Tanner worked. Admittedly, I smuggled him into work a few times too. I loved heading out to play catch with the beast of a dog whenever I had a lull or a break. And I supposed in many ways, Mom was right. He'd become as much my dog as Tanner's.

She headed to the back door after I'd nodded, and proceeded to open it. I considered throwing her a warning, but decided to sit back and watch instead. I couldn't be held responsible for reverting to a more immature me when my parents were around.

On cue, Rex barged through the open doorway, taking Mom by complete surprise as he made to barrel between her legs. No easy feat when Rex was barely a foot shorter than her.

I burst into laughter as Mom found herself sitting on Rex's back. For a moment she balanced precariously, as though she was starring in a Rhodesian rodeo, before Rex dipped and scooted through, leaving Mom reaching for the wall to steady herself. In just those few seconds, she looked windswept and suitably flustered. My snorted laughter snapped her gaze in my direction, and my continued hollers of laughter were enough to bring Dad and Tanner back to the room, and for Mom to throw me a look that could kill.

"Carter Francis, you little sh—"

Tears rolled down my cheeks and I clutched my gut. I'd inherited my lack of swearing from my mom, but like me, when the mood took her, she'd have a lapse and all manner of cussing would spill forth. And every time it did, I would end up collapsed on the floor and gasping for breath from my amusement.

"—you knew he would do that, you rotten—"

It was too much. My stomach hurt, cramps forming as I struggled to breathe, laughter spilling over, but making me sound like I was deranged.

"—toad. You think that's funny? Just you wait till I tell Tanner what I caught you doing when you were sixteen with that Ken doll."

My laughter stopped abruptly and I gasped in horror. She may as well have threatened to cut off my balls and been an inch away from doing it, my reaction was that quick. "You wouldn't?"

She stood in the open doorway, hair disheveled, arms crossed over her chest, and looking so happy with herself. I looked at her and then at Tanner, knowing he'd heard her. How could he not have? It was time to act fast. "I'll tell Aunt Betsy what really happened to the candlesticks that were 'damaged' when you moved." I'd pulled out the big guns as I eyed her warily, wondering how far she'd take this.

Mom's eyes rounded, growing as big as saucers as we stared each other off. She opened her mouth to speak but Dad's voice got there first. "All righty then, and welcome to the family, Tanner." I heard a small thud-like sound, as if Dad was giving Tanner a commiserative pat on the back. I would have looked, but there was no chance I was letting Mom out of my line of sight just yet. She was standing right by the fruit bowl, and everybody knows fruit's just ammunition. I seriously would not put it past her.

Tanner's laughter swept over me, melting my tense shoulders a little and reminding me I was supposed to be the sane one. If this carried on, I'd only have myself to blame if after this week he decided to run. "Okay." He clapped his hands, humor evident just in that single word. "Is it safe to cut through and start the grill?"

Mom recovered quicker than I did. She patted

down her hair and smiled sweetly. "Of course, Tanner. Lead the way and I'll help. It'll give us the chance to have a chat."

I focused hard on my mom, willing her to look again in my direction, trying to warn her to not appear insane, and to please God, not share the Ken doll story.

———

IT WAS MIDWEEK AND HAD BEEN A PRETTY CRAPPY ONE at that, at least work wise, and I was desperate to get home. Monday I'd had to put Mr. Pollack's sweet dog, Bessie, to sleep, which was a heartache; Tuesday I'd felt decidedly uncomfortable when Scott had started the process of internal reviews, which meant he'd breathed down my neck during an operation and a couple of appointments; and to top things off, there was a new e-mail from Denver. He had already delayed his return once, making my time at the hospital increasingly uncomfortable with Scott's cutting remarks and looks of disgust once more becoming a regular occurrence, but the e-mail sneering at me from my inbox left me catching my breath. Denver was officially retiring and had announced Scott as the official manager, and new director, since he was apparently buying into the business.

Lauren had given me a smile of commiseration when just before we'd attempted to leave work that night, Scott had called the whole team for an impromptu meeting. She didn't know the full extent of Scott's bigotry, but she was observant enough to know that something wasn't right between the two of us.

Since that one time at the bar months earlier, nothing as blatant had happened, which was a relief. There'd been no more cancellations, no outward vile remarks. But his looks, his tone, his general attitude when "dealing" with me, as truly that was what it felt like, as though I was an inconvenience, made work a challenge. I was no longer as eager to start the day, becoming increasingly anxious and frustrated by the hostility I would encounter.

Across the room, I watched as Scott smugly announced his new appointment and accepted the congratulatory backslaps and handshakes. I couldn't not reach out to shake his hand and offer a nod of congrats. The difficulty was the rest of the staff liked him. The self-assured turd had charmed them all into believing he was a good guy. But I knew so much better.

I struggled to not flinch when he gripped my hand just a little too tightly and fought hard not to then wipe his touch from my palm. This guy was a creep. He gave Joffrey, the psycho from *Game of Thrones*, a run for his money. Admittedly that was probably a slight exaggeration unless of course Scott headed home to kill and maim, but still, he left me wanting to scrub his nastiness off me.

I headed back toward the door, ready to exit as soon as was appropriate to do so, Lauren close on my heels. Coming up beside me, she pinched the skin at my waist, causing me to flinch. "Hey!" I glanced down to her and was immediately confused by her raised brows. "What?"

"Did you not hear?"

I shook my head. "Hear what?" All I wanted to do was to leave, head home to where I knew my mom was cooking my favorite, and cuddle up with Tanner before I sucked him off.

"Drinks on Friday."

I tilted my head and frowned. "Who, us?" I couldn't remember her arranging anything with me.

"Nope." She shook her head and then indicated with a small flick in the direction of Scott. "The new big man expects us all to be available on Friday for celebratory drinks."

My stomach dipped. There was no way I was going to give up any of my free time to Scott.

"It's compulsory."

I snorted. "How does he figure that?" I whisper-hissed. Who the heck did this douche think he was? Nobody could make heading out for drinks compulsory.

"It's at twelve thirty, so still in work time. He's shutting up shop, and has a couple of on-call doctors available." Her tone was low as she shared this with me. How could I have not heard Scott say anything?

I groaned. "You're serious, right?"

With a scrunch of her nose, Lauren nodded. "As a heart attack." She placed her hand on my forearm and gave me a small squeeze. "At least you finish work early on Fridays though, so you can start your weekend before the rest of us suckers."

This was true. There was a small ray of light at least.

"Better than hanging out with some of these boring blockheads." She threw me a wide smirk and I laughed loudly.

"Shh," I attempted while laughing. One of these days, Lauren and her smart mouth were going to get fired.

She threw me a conspiratorial wink and grinned. "We'll be all right. I've got your back."

Admittedly, her words did make me feel better. Considering we hadn't known each other all that long, she could already read some of my tells and one of those was knowing when I was anxious. I was lucky to have her. Over the years people had failed pretty spectacularly to read me correctly. On face value, I seemed like a guy who had it all together. My six feet was nothing to scoff at. I wasn't a waif exactly, so most thought I could handle myself, and that along with my education and profession made it all too easy for people to form expectations of my personality, my physical abilities, my overall confidence.

While I was far from a coward, the thought of a fight left me feeling sick to my stomach. And while my height and build would suggest I wasn't a shrinking violet and was possibly a man's man—whatever the heck that really meant—I wore my heart on my damn sleeve and was known to break down watching *ET*. Okay, so literally every single time that one scene between Elliot and ET brought me to my knees and dragged tears from my traitorous tear ducts. But most people didn't see this, and it meant that far too often I was faced with ignorance. Especially when it came to my sexuality.

At least once a week I "came out," even in a smaller town like mine. There was never a first, and I couldn't ever imagine a world when there would be a last time. That being the case, I was sure there was the expectation that if someone wasn't "okay" or "comfortable" with my sexuality, with me, I was expected to simply suck it up and not let them impact my life.

There were days when I was tired of my false grin. Tired of having to suck it up because of people's stupidity. And Lauren, she was getting an inkling of the real me. That was kind of reassuring, especially since she was the only person, apart from Tanner, who I'd gotten to know since relocating.

I grinned at Lauren. "Thanks. I've got yours too. I can pull a mean wedgie when needed. I've even been known to pull out the big guns and curse like a sailor should the occasion demand it." I threw her a wink at the same time I realized the meeting was finally over.

Her snort-laugh was loud as she all but pushed me out of the room and ushered me toward the exit. As we reached her car, she turned and looked at me, a wicked smirk on her face. "New plan."

My shoulders sagged with my immediate suspicion. "What?"

"Get that hunk of yours to drop you off on Friday morning and pick you up from the bar."

That was not a good idea, so immediately I shook my head.

Lauren nodded. "Yes! Didn't you hear Scott say the credit card was going behind the bar? He droned on for at least five hundred hours about staff morale and bonding." She snorted. "We're totally taking advantage as, let's be honest here, out of the dicks we work with, he's the biggest, and I'm absolutely not talking about the one between his legs."

I shook my head at her, both amused and terrified about not only her suggestion but the thought of Scott's penis. I considered gagging for a moment. "I don't kn—"

"Yes. Listen, I have no idea what his problem is, but I've seen the way he treats you. Nothing so bad as to raise too many brows, but he's... I don't know... different. And since we can't tell him to fuck off without getting fired, we'll just get drunk by drinking booze he's paying for." She stood on her tiptoes and planted a loud kiss on my cheek. "Tell Tanner you'll call for a lift on Friday from the bar." Without another word, she jumped in her car and flew out of the parking lot, leaving me walking slowly toward my car and wondering what she was getting me into.

It didn't take long to get home, have a quick shower, and be sitting around the table with my three favorite people. We were halfway through Mom's lamb roast when Tanner mentioned a delivery for the patio doors coming in on Friday, and I groaned, remembering what else was happening on that day.

His firm hand landed on my thigh, and he squeezed lightly. When my gaze landed on his, he tilted his head in concern. "What's that groan for? Something wrong?"

With the release of a deep breath, I placed my hand on his, finding comfort in his touch. "Sort of, well, not really." His brows lifted at my response. "It's just Denver definitely isn't returning, so Scott is stepping into his position permanently, plus he's buying into the practice, and to top that load of crappiness off, we all have to attend this company morale drinks get-together on Friday afternoon during work hours so there's no getting out of it." By the time I'd finished, Tanner was wide-eyed, yet still managed to look a mixture of annoyed and concerned.

He remained quiet at my splurge of information. I had no idea what he was thinking. Mom interrupted the quiet that was beginning to feel uncomfortable. "Oh, that's a shame about your boss. You like him, right?"

I nodded at her, distracted and feeling increasingly uneasy about Tanner's nonverbal reaction. "Yeah, he was a good guy and good at his job."

"That's a pity. It seems this Scott person who's taking his place is making a positive effort though, wanting to get employees together." She paused, which was unlike her, and was enough to drag my attention away from Tanner. Her gaze flicked at Tanner and then me; she was far too observant and was no doubt aware something was going on. "So, what's the problem with Scott then? He's not cut out for the role?"

"No, he's not." Tanner's voice was deep and serious. His hand tightened a little on my leg, and my eyes immediately met his. "He's a little-dick bigot." He seemed to remember himself and moved his gaze to my parents. "Sorry," he offered, "but after all the BS he threw at Carter when he first took over, he doesn't deserve a civil word."

I clenched my jaw. I knew Tanner was looking out for me, and I loved him more for it, but it must have been clear to him from my mom's questions that I hadn't told her anything about Scott and what had happened. I didn't need my parents worrying about me. Christ, I was a grown man with a mom who too often forgot that. The last thing I wanted was to give her any ammunition.

"It's fine." I cut in before he could continue or my mom could start. "There've been no dramas for a while now, not since that night." Despite my annoyance, heat crept up my neck and to my cheeks when I recalled the significance of that night for Tanner and me. It was enough to get his own jaw relaxing a little and a small leer to lift his lips. "It's fine," I asserted. I hadn't yet dared a glance at my parents, but I knew there was no avoiding it.

Mom's face was tight, and pink colored her cheeks. Yes, my mom could be fierce, especially when it came to protecting me. "Mom," I attempted. "Honestly, it's not a big deal."

With narrowed eyes on me for a few seconds, she then zeroed in on Tanner. "Talk. Tell me exactly what this little-dick bigot did to my baby." I opened my mouth to intervene, but without looking, she managed to shut me down. "You, zip it." Her eyes remained firmly on Tanner. "Spill."

And he did, much to my groans of embarrassment, and my desire to crawl into a hole and wonder how my mom was still able to make me feel this way despite being almost thirty, owning a house, and being a doctor. I couldn't sit through it all, so I started clearing away the plates while feeling so relieved I hadn't told Tanner about the daily scowls or the harsh tones. And while at times it felt like I was in a hellish version of high school, which was far too close to how mine had been with the way Scott behaved, I certainly wasn't. I'd chosen the easy road admittedly, or the hard road, depending on how you looked at it. But choosing to ignore it all meant that I could do my job. It also meant that I tried my hardest to ignore Scott and his hatred. It had been sort of working. Until now.

"So"—my dad's voice surprised me and made me stop loading the dishwasher. He'd been silent through everything—"what are you doing about it?" I looked across at him and realized his eyes were firmly on me. "I'm confused as to why you'd ever allow someone to treat you this way." My gut clenched at the disappointment painting his words. "You have people around you who love you, who'll support you with every decision you make, so what are you going to do?"

Embarrassment pushed me forward. "My decision was to move on and ignore it since nothing else has happened. So…" I paused. "This, right here, is all of you supporting my decision, right?" I was being a butthole, but the disappointment radiating off all three people I cared about had me digging deeper. I raised my brows and looked at the three of them, all looking various stages of frustrated. My eyes finally rested on Tanner. He looked pissed, but then, so was I.

"Right, thought so," I huffed. "The dishes are done and I'm turning in for the night." My gaze drifted from Tanner, too mortified not only by the discussion, but my behavior, yet still, with my emotions high, I forged forward, nodded, and left the room.

About thirty minutes later, after hushed voices and scraped chairs, I heard the front door open and then close. I looked at the empty side of my bed and groaned, wanting to smack myself silly for my over-reaction. The funny thing about feelings though, was that far too often rational thought had no say.

CHAPTER SEVENTEEN

TANNER

Un-fucking-believable. I shook my head as I walked to the couch and passed Davis another beer. "He's so fuckin' stubborn. I swear I need to tan his fucking hide...." *before kissing it better.* I flopped down on the well-worn cushions and cursed at myself. I was hopeless, and Carter was as hot as he was unbelievably fucking pig-headed.

Davis snorted. "So you keep saying." I glanced at him, throwing him a pissed-off look. "Hey." He raised one hand in surrender. "You're the bastard who dragged me out of bed just so you could bitch about Carter, on repeat." He took a pull of his beer. "You know, you've said the word stubborn twelve times now, and variations of fuck seventeen."

The throw cushion I flung hit him square in the

face, leaving me with a hint of satisfaction and Davis spluttering.

"What the fuck, dude!" He shook his head and wiped at his beer-splattered tee. "Wind your asshole in, yeah?"

A drop of guilt hit me. I had dragged his ass out of bed so I could vent, after all. With a sigh, I rubbed my palm over my face. I was tired and confused, and frustrated. "Sorry," I begrudgingly offered.

"Look." I cast an apologetic glance at Davis when he spoke. "I get that you're all loved up and this is your first fight, but seriously, dude, what the fuck are you still doing here?"

I kept my face neutral, annoyed that he was right, and wondering why I'd allowed Carter to run me out. "You know—" I raised a brow and threw as much attitude as possible at him as I continued, "You just said 'dude' twice."

Davis snorted and barely held on to his mouthful of beer. Clearing his throat, he gave me the bird. "Just fuck off already and go and kiss and make up. He was pissed because you tattled on him like a pussy." I made to speak, but he threw me a warning glance. "You did, deal with it. Then he overreacted and got all Beyoncé on you."

My brows furrowed. I had no fucking clue what he was talking about.

"What?" He had the nerve to look confused.

"What the heck does Beyoncé have to do with anything, and since when have you listened to Beyoncé?"

Davis rolled his eyes as he released an exasperated breath. "Whatever, dickwad. She's got a great ass, and you know I like asses. Just... he was embarrassed and dealt with it badly, and you, genius, did a runner."

"I didn't do—"

"Yeah, you did. I know you've been staying together almost every fucking night." It was true. We lived in each other's pockets, and I liked it that way. "So, let me ask you this." He looked far too cocky as he waited for what I assumed was my full attention. Seemingly he thought he had it, since he asked, "If you were really planning on going home and not heading back to lover boy's bed, where the fuck is your monster of a dog?"

"Fucker." My response was instant because the bastard was right. I huffed out a breath, knowing I needed to get my ass into gear and head back to Carter.

This whole thing was ridiculous. Obviously

Davis knew it, I knew it, and I was hoping Carter would realize it too. There was only one way to find out, and that was to stop being a fool and go and talk it out with Carter.

This whole relationship stuff was as confusing as it was amazing. And Davis was right. It was our first argument, if you could even call it that. My shoulders stiffened, my eyes widened as a thought popped into my head. My eyes shifted to Davis's, his laughter drawing me to him.

"You're so fucking dick-whipped, dude." He didn't give me the chance to even comment on his third use of a word that I was certain he hadn't used for fifteen years. "You just figured make-up sex was on the horizon, huh?"

My lips twitched, because once again, the bastard known as my best friend was on the ball. I stood, finished my beer, and then tapped him on the shoulder as I walked by.

"Yeah, be off with you, and don't come back."

I grinned as I dropped my bottle in the outside recycling bin on my way out. Once in my truck and on the way back to Carter's, I shifted uncomfortably in my seat. My dick twitched at the thought of taking Carter hard, then washing him thoroughly in the shower and going down on him.

I was sure he wouldn't need much convincing. Time would tell, I supposed.

A few minutes later, I switched off the engine, cut the lights, and headed to the front of the house. The door was unlocked. I entered quietly, not wanting to wake his folks. Just as I made my way to the staircase, I heard a scrape of a stool coming from the kitchen. I paused, then turned and headed in the direction. I opened the door to find Carter standing next to the kitchen counter. His hands gripped the edge, and his gaze immediately settled on mine.

I entered the room, closing the door quietly behind me. I took a couple of steps forward and then paused, giving myself a moment to rake my eyes over his body. He looked tired. I knew it was late, something like one in the morning, and I also knew he had to work in a few hours. But what struck me the hardest and had my feet moving was the pink touching the tops of his cheeks, the slight sheen in his eyes, and the way he bit his bottom lip.

He was upset.

Fuck.

As I stepped to the edge of the countertop, rounding on him, he immediately moved away from the stool. His arms flung around my waist just as I scooped him close and tugged him into my arms.

"I'm so sorry." His voice was whisper soft and filled with such emotion that I squeezed him tighter.

"Shh… it's okay, baby."

"No, it's not." His face brushed across my chest as he shook his head. "I was so out of order. I can't believe you left. Then you were gone. You weren't here. Mom and Dad are giving me the silent treatment and throwing me looks like they're disappointed in me, and I let you go." He sniffed, and I hoped to God he wasn't crying.

"Hey." I pressed a kiss on top of his head. "I love you." His head brushed across my chest as he lifted his face. When his eyes finally met mine, I spotted the pink, but there were no tears. Thank Christ. I was sure if he cried, I'd be offering the goddamn world to get him to stop. "It's okay. Let's just go to bed."

"You're staying?" Brightness filled his eyes, hope lighting them. He looked so fucking adorable.

"Yeah," I answered with a grin. "Not going anywhere, okay?"

He nodded. "I am sorry though. I know I overreacted."

"You did," I agreed. I then laughed at his wide-eyed expression. "What? I'm just agreeing with you."

His eyes squinted a little. "I know, but you didn't have to agree right away or anything."

I laughed a little harder.

"Fine," he sighed, "I know I did, but you were pushing—"

"Because I care."

"I know." He nodded, his lips finally tugging up. "And I'm glad you do, but you can be so pushy, and stubborn, and all growly and stuff over me."

My brows lifted in amusement. "Growly?"

"Yes." He rolled his eyes. "You get all demanding and macho, and don't get me wrong, it's hot and everything, but, Tanner, you told on me to my parents."

I pressed my lips together, trying to contain my laughter. Apparently I didn't do such a great job as Carter ended up saying, "And it's not funny."

I may have snorted.

"I'm serious." He pushed at my chest.

I grabbed hold of his hands and wrapped him back in my arms, my laughter breaking free at the same time. "Listen," I managed to say around the chuckle spilling forth, "let's just get to bed, let me take care of you, and we'll deal with your tattletale issues tomorrow." He struggled a little in my arms. Unable to move, he bit my chest. "Ouch!" I laughed.

"If anyone bites, it's going to be me, yeah? You know, when I'm being all macho and shit."

He bit again, but this time his small snicker touched my ears. My chest felt lighter at the sound, and I was almost lightheaded at the thought of truly taking care of Carter and putting all this bull behind us.

"Right." I ducked down, and before Carter had the opportunity to react or figure out what I was going to do, I pushed my shoulder against his stomach and lifted him. He flipped over my shoulder with an oomph and a loud laugh, and I held on, racing upstairs with him in a fireman's lift.

As we went past the spare room, I smacked his ass and shushed him, my reminder for him to be quiet. He grunted and pinched my ass cheeks in response. We carried on to his room, and I was never more relieved that it was at the opposite side of the house, with a couple of rooms separating us from his parents.

I needed to make Carter scream.

THE MORNING LIGHT SPILLED THROUGH THE curtains, and I drew Carter closer, not quite ready to get up yet. He stirred, and I smiled at him, then brushed my lips over his. "Morning."

"Morning," he breathed before stretching into me and groaning.

"You okay?"

He hummed in response. "Deliciously sore."

I moaned at the visual of a writhing Carter and captured his mouth in a heated kiss, immediately needing his lips. The image of last night and pounding into him was too close to the surface to ignore. After forcing myself to pull away, I asked, "Too sore?" I searched his eyes, waiting for his honest answer.

"Well," he said with a laugh, "it depends on what you have planned."

Casting my gaze over his face and then chest, I then lifted the sheets, my eyes landing on his erection. "Well, I am hun—"

"Knock, knock." Two sharp taps on the door interrupted us and had us separating like we'd been caught making out by, yeah, Carter's mom. I snorted as Carter fumbled with the sheet, his cheeks heated and his eyes wide as he stared at the door.

He closed his lids briefly before calling out, "Yeah?" His voice was higher pitched than normal, causing me to snort quietly and earning me a smack on my chest.

"Ooh, you're up." I snorted a little louder when Carter threw a look of disbelief at the door. "Do you have time for breakfast before work? You're in bed a little later than usual."

He groaned. "Err, just toast, Mom, thanks. Give me five."

There was a moment of silence before his mom spoke again. "But didn't Tanner come back?"

I chuckled. "Morning," I greeted loudly.

"Morning, Tanner. So you'll need more than five minutes, I assume."

I cast an amused glance at Carter who'd turned a brilliant shade of red. "No, no...," he half muttered, half stumbled.

"Nonsense," she continued. "I remember what your dad was like at your age. He had quite the stamina and appetite. There was this one ti—"

Carter shot out of bed at the same time he yelled "No!" He grabbed a towel off the linen basket and was wrapping it around himself as he opened the door just a crack. "Mom, seriously, toast is good. I'm going to be late otherwise."

He stood at the door, his muscles tense, one hand gripping the towel, the other on the door. Amusement danced in my gut, and I was so tempted to rile him up and make the situation so much more awkward. His reaction if I were to sidle up to the side of him, out of the view of the door, and start playing with his sexy-as-fuck ass was difficult to resist. I shifted on the bed, in half a mind to do just that, but my movement caused Carter to swing his head around to face me. He squinted immediately, sending me a silent order to stop exactly where I was.

I threw him a big-ass grin as laughter caught in my throat. I edged closer to the bed, knowing full well when I stood, I'd be on show for his eyes only, sticking out for his... admittedly, for my own amusement.

As I swung my legs over the side of the bed, his eyes widened, jaw tensing. "Thanks, Mom. Ten minutes." He quickly closed the door, leaving behind his mom's trailing laughter.

It took longer than ten minutes before a frazzled Carter was pulling on his pants and grabbing a slice of cold toast as he raced out the door. I laughed, watching him leave, feeling so relieved that I'd had time to put an extra-large grin on his face this morning.

After our ridiculous nonargument of yesterday,

as Carter had dubbed it, the sex had been pretty fucking epic. I was more than happy if every stupid half-assed disagreement ended up with us sorting everything out so quickly and shooting our loads.

Yeah, it was how every day should end and start as far as I was concerned. Well, except for the bullshit.

"So"—Marcy sidled up next to me—"you sorted everything out last night then?"

I nodded and shared a cautious smile with her. While she was super easygoing and seemed supportive of our relationship, interacting with any parent had alarm bells ringing. It wasn't something I was exactly used to. "Yeah."

"Good job." She patted my arm tenderly. "You're good for him." My brows lifted in surprise. "He's so calm and doesn't like to unsettle the waters. He's always been the same. Don't get me wrong. He has a backbone and knows how to stand up for himself." I nodded at that, not imagining he would have been given much option to be any other way with a mom like Marcy. "But he would also prefer to fly under the radar and make the best of the situation."

"Is that a bad thing?" I asked as I closed the front door and we both headed to the kitchen. It was actually something I admired about Carter. He gave head and smiled widely. Laughter still bubbled in my chest, and my throat was raw, but after the week I'd had both were welcome.

"You need a drink now?" Her words held every trace of her amusement. She leaned onto the bar and signaled the bartender. When she looked back at me, she quirked her brow in question.

"Sure." I gave in. "But just the one."

With a quick wink at me, Lauren ordered us drinks. She was a good friend, who truly kept me sane, especially ever since Scott had come on the scene. I glanced around the bar, seeking the guy out.

It didn't take long before my eyes landed on him. Scott was talking to one of the young nurses, his hip resting against the bar. It was funny how such a good-looking man was so damned ugly. I supposed that's what hate did though. It bred ugliness, pushed it through veins until it reached part of a person's soul. That was definitely the case with Scott.

Just as I was about to look away, hearing Lauren say thanks to the bar staff, Scott's eyes met mine. I froze, eyes widening when his gaze roamed my face and an expression I couldn't quite place lit his features. Clenching my jaw at the absurdity of being forced to be at the stupid bar by a man who loathed me, I dragged my eyes away and reached out for the drink Lauren held out to me. I downed the contents in one, feeling the burn of the liquor as it raced down my throat.

"Wow, Carter. That wasn't intended to be a shot."

I flicked my eyes to hers and saw concern on her face. With a forced smile, I bobbed my head, trying to conjure some words. I needed to leave and get home to Tanner.

That thought was enough to center me, and my mouth relaxed into a more natural smile. Home and Tanner sounded perfect. While my place technically wasn't home to him, I had every hope that one day it would be.

"Thanks, honey. But you know what, I'm going to head home." Screw the time. I'd deal with any BS ramifications on Monday.

Her brows dipped as she reached out and took the empty glass from my hand. "You sure?"

"Yep." I nodded. "I'm just going to head to the restroom and… crap, I don't have my car. I'll send Tanner a text. It shouldn't take him long."

"Okay. I'll say goodbye now though. Harriet's calling me over." Lauren kissed me on the cheek and walked away. It was time to bail.

I texted Tanner while heading to the bathroom. He shot back a text immediately, saying he'd be ten

"Listen, Scott." I looked up at the dusting of clouds littering the sky above, giving myself a moment to get my head together. Finally, I focused on the man before me. He appeared broken, so much more than my initial assessment of sad. Did he deserve to be miserable after everything he'd done? A part of me nodded in righteousness. But the man before me wasn't the cocksure Scott who'd been a homophobic prick. "I have no idea what's going on, or who filed the report—" He made to speak, but I shook my head before continuing. "It should have been me. I should have made a complaint the first time you were... inappropriate, but I didn't.

"I have no idea what's going on with you, and it's none of my business, but—"

"I'm gay."

I was sure at the moment I looked like a caricature of an old Warner Brothers' cartoon with my eyes springing out of their sockets. It was the last thing I expected to fall out of his mouth. *What the fuck!* It was a swear-worthy moment.

I clamped my mouth shut and then made to speak, but nothing came to mind. Scott stared at me in abject horror. I had no idea if he'd intended to come out to me or not, but from his wide and glassy eyes, I assumed the latter.

"I…." He shook his head and blanched. "I…. That's the first time…."

"The first time you said it aloud," I prompted.

He nodded, his rounded eyes not leaving mine. A flush covered his cheeks before he suddenly paled. "I think I'm going to throw up."

Crap. I stepped into his space and placed my hand on his back, encouraging him to bend forward. "Breathe." I inhaled and exhaled exaggerated breaths, encouraging him to do the same. With my palm still on his back, I glanced around, looking for somewhere he could sit. Spotting a crate to the side, I ushered Scott over and maneuvered him to take a seat. He did so in silence.

"You're going to be okay." The platitude was already out there, and I grimaced at the emptiness of the words. It was too late to take it back, so I continued, despite the rush of emotion and confusion flooding me. "I know it doesn't feel that way, but this is a good thing, scary as hell, but good."

Scott lifted his gaze to mine. Some color had returned to his face. Disbelief played in his eyes, but I also spotted something else, something more. Hope. "It is," I continued with a little more conviction. "For whatever reason you waited until now, at this juncture in your life, everything

CHAPTER NINETEEN

TANNER

When I'd first spotted Carter with Scott in the alley, the need to charge in and get Carter away from potential harm had been fierce. It had waged a battle in me, and it had taken everything in me for rational thought to take control and remind me that Carter was a grown-ass man who could take care of himself. That brief hesitation had allowed me to read the situation better.

Seeing Scott sitting with his head between his legs, Carter before him speaking just loud enough for me to hear fragments, was enough for me to take stock and rein my hothead in. Just.

I gripped Carter's hand and settled it on my thigh as we drove to my place. We wouldn't stay there the night as Carter's parents were at his, plus there was my dog to take care of, who'd taken permanent residence at Carter's. But I could read Carter well enough to know he needed to talk through whatever had gone down today. That, and I needed to know what had happened.

When we pulled up outside my place, Carter smiled at me, gratitude evident. I pressed a kiss to his hand and released him, got out and headed to the front door. He quickly caught up with me and leaned against my back, cheek resting on the back of my neck as I unlocked and opened the door.

"Beer or water?" I asked once inside. "Sorry, I have nothing else." I shook my head—even my refrigerator was bare, apart from out-of-date condiments. Over the past few weeks, I'd virtually lived at Carter's. Neither of us had questioned the steady move of my clothes into his closet, but I knew at some point we'd have to chat about it. It wasn't the time though.

"Beer's good. Thanks."

I headed into the kitchen while Carter made his way to the sofa in the sitting room. A moment later, I sat beside him, my knee touching his thigh as I turned to face him better. "You ready to tell me what that was all about?"

He shook his head in wide-eyed wonder. "I have

whole situation. I wasn't a complete asshole that I couldn't understand the fear of someone coming out, but after the nightmare he'd put Carter through, I couldn't forgive or forget so easily.

"But you didn't see how much he was hurting, Tanner." He gripped my hand tightly when I told him what a turd I thought Scott was.

"I get that." Admittedly not fully. I had no idea who Scott really was. It seemed the guy didn't know himself either. "I just can't believe you invited him over to ou— your house tomorrow, that's all." Carter's eyes softened, but I chose to ignore his reaction.

"Don't you think it's odd— No, not odd, I mean terrifying and… sad that a guy his age has the need to not only stay hidden but to go a step further and behave the way he did toward me?" He shook his head, face straight, and emotion heavy in his eyes.

Fuck me, this man was going to be the death of me. "You kill me, you know?" He tilted his head in confusion, so I continued. "You're so kind and forgiving, hell… trusting. I'm not sure I'll ever be good enough to deserve you." I meant every word. Carter had me tied up in knots, had done since day one when I'd found him butt-naked and trapped.

He smiled widely and stroked his thumb over my

hand. "You're more than enough, Tanner." He paused a moment. I watched closely as his lips twisted a little and he started chewing on his bottom lip. With a small clearing of his throat, he said, "I think he needs help, or at least to talk to someone who knows the truth. It's the reason why I invited him over to *our* place."

THE NEXT MORNING, WE WERE UP EARLY SAYING goodbye to Carter's folks. The week had gone by crazy fast, not only filled with our usual day-to-day living and working, but with the drama and outing of Scott.

I'd admitted to Carter, as I'd dragged his ass out of bed, that I would be glad when the day was finally over so we could shut ourselves away from the world. Not only would I have to be on my best behavior with Scott, which rubbed me the wrong way, but all I wanted to do was work out the logistics of moving myself in officially.

Carter had laughed when I'd whined earlier this morning saying I just wanted to get shit done. Though when he'd straddled my face and then taken hold of my erection with his mouth, my complaints

CHAPTER TWENTY

CARTER

We were finally back at home. We'd just dumped a suitcase filled with clothes in the spare room, and Tanner was virtually dragging me to the shower.

I went willingly, needing the escapism only Tanner could offer me. It had been a weird day.

Not only had I promised to fuck—I cleared my throat at the word and the image it evoked, and hoped to Christ I'd do it right—Tanner, something I was desperate albeit anxious to do, but also Scott had visited and survived.

It was awkward as hell, which was to be expected, and we didn't get into the ins and outs of his life or his secrets. But by the end of breakfast, I'd lost count of how many times he'd apologized. Heck,

Tanner had even stepped in and told him enough, and that the apologies needed to stop.

Scott had also sent in his resignation, and I wasn't quite sure how I felt about that. It wasn't like I expected to be Scott's best pal or anything, but from what I'd seen of him over breakfast, he actually seemed like a decent guy. Tanner did repeatedly remind me though that he was sure Scott didn't even know who he was, so the jury was still out.

I jumped, lost in thought when Tanner tugged my T-shirt over my head. I grinned at his enthusiasm. He told me often enough that he wanted me to top, and while I'd felt a little selfish for pulling back and not giving him my all, I knew he'd wait, despite not knowing my reasons.

It was time to fess up.

Both naked after fumbling to undress each other, we stepped into the shower and under the warm spray. Tanner's mouth settled against my lips, his breathing heavy as he devoured mine. His tongue was slick and warm as it gently probed my mouth. I pushed against him eagerly, stroking my own tongue against his before pulling back for air.

"You okay?" His voice was deep and breathy.

"Yeah." I nodded as his eyes searched mine.

"You don't ha—"

With two fingers inside, stretching, scissoring, and working him over, I leaned forward and traced his belly button with kisses, working my way to one of his taut nipples. I sucked deeply, earning a satisfying groan. When I released with a pop, I lapped at the area, teasing his nipple. His hand clamped on to the back of my head.

"Fuck, baby. I need your mouth."

Searing heat threatened to consume me as my lips met his. So lost in his tongue, his gentle caress of my own, followed by the growing intensity traveling through my veins, it was only his needy groans that kept my fingers moving. With three fingers now deep inside him, I tilted them lightly and almost came when Tanner tore his lips from mine and gasped loudly. He was thrusting erratically against my fingers. I had to get inside him before it was all over.

His large hands gripped my arms and our eyes connected. Desperation had never looked so fucking hot. Need dripped off every syllable when he said, "Carter, I swear to fucking God—"

I leaned back, removing my fingers at the same time. As he closed his eyes, I said, "Baby, I got you." And I did.

With a quick slather of lube on my aching cock, a

stroke of his balls for good measure, which earned me another delicious groan, I pressed against his puckered entrance.

My thighs shook. While nerves still slid through me, it was lust that rode me hard, that and a need to make everything perfect for the man before me. I'd told him countless times how much I loved him, but this was different, more visceral, a more perfect way of showing him exactly how deeply my love for him burned.

I breached him slowly, carefully, holding back my desire to thrust.

"Carter." I dragged my eyes from our connection to his eyes. "Fuck me. Please." The desperation was still there, but it was his eyes and the love held in them that had me plunging deeply.

A guttural moan escaped me when I bottomed out. His heat clamped down tightly on my hardness, and the moment was a contender for the most perfect moment we'd shared. As I pulled back, only to drive back in, I grinned widely at him.

"What?" he asked breathlessly, a grin curving his mouth.

"It's as perfect as our first time."

Tanner bit down on his bottom lip and closed his eyes briefly as I surged in and out once more. His something romantic like a candlelit dinner, or cutesy like… whatever the heck couples gave each other that was cute.

Taking a step toward him, I stretched out my hand for him to take. He did so without hesitation, which surprised me. I expected him to put up more of a fight. I pulled him into my arms and planted a kiss on his warm lips. I sighed happily on contact, but there was no way I would take it further, not with his kickass surprise waiting.

"Should I be nervous, because I am?" He looked skeptically at me.

Taking his hand, I led him out of the kitchen and to the staircase. As we climbed the stairs, I could barely contain myself. "I love you. And I think it's important to accept every part of each other, warts, kinks, and all." I felt him hesitate, so I pushed on, virtually tugging him up the remaining steps. When we reached our bedroom door, I paused to allow the word "kink" to settle in. I also paused to work out the best move. I knew I may need a quick escape, but I also desperately wanted to see his reaction.

"Just open the stupid door already."

Not wanting to push him too far, I moved to the side so I could open the door, with him entering next to me.

"You ready?"

"Do I have a choice?"

I grinned. "Kinks and all," I murmured next to his ear as I pushed the door open wide, put my hand on his lower back, and forced him to take a couple of steps in.

Flickering candlelight greeted us. I nodded in appreciation at the mood lighting. My gaze then followed his, but while he stood frozen in abject horror, mine landed on the first display with glee. Two Ken dolls were strategically placed on the end of the bed, both butt naked, and in the 69 position.

Then I caught Carter's head flicking to another display; this one I was mighty proud of. Three Kens were going at it in a sort of triangle, one impressively taking it up the ass while he was giving head to the other cockless Ken. It had taken at least ten minutes to get those bastards to behave. Thank Christ for superglue.

"Ta-da!" I considered doing jazz hands but didn't want to overdo it. "You know"—I stepped up behind Carter and wrapped my arms around him, deliberately locking his arms to his sides in case he decided to strike out—"I think I can totally get why you'd use Ken dolls as porn." He tried to spin around in my arms and made a disgruntled sound that may have

Damn, he was right. That made me feel ancient, and I was so far from that shit it wasn't funny.

Carter nodded. "Absolutely, you know we love having Libby over. Though—" He paused and looked me up and down, his brows pulling together. *The hell?* "—I'm not sure you could handle it anymore."

I threw a look his way, not at all impressed with his truths. Carter smiled and blinked innocently at me. So many blinks so damn close together was not natural, though I supposed he looked kinda cute doing it. *Asswipe.*

"For shit's sake, I'm only thirty-five."

Along with a shrug, Carter's smile turned into a grin. "So in that case, what are you waiting for? Live a little. You know, go and see if you can get a life beyond that sweet girl of yours."

"I've got a life," I grumbled. And I did, sort of. Admittedly it involved me juggling owning and running my business, keeping house, and most importantly being the best dad possible. That shit right there took time. Considering there was barely time to shit, sleep, or even jerk off, how in the hell could I handle more than I already had?

"I know you do." Carter reached out and placed his hand on my forearm, squeezing lightly. "You have a pretty amazing life, but you know—"

"You need to get laid."

"Tanner," Carter admonished at the same time that I groaned. "I was trying to be subtle. You know, go for tact, ease in gently?"

Tanner grinned, and I rolled my eyes at the pair of them. "Tact was never this dick's forte; you'll soon get used to it, Carter. And I'm fine." I was aiming for neutral, reassured, perhaps even as though I was in control. But fuck me, I did really need to get laid.

In all seriousness, it had been well before Libby's birth since the last time I'd got any. I had a serious case of blue balls and a constantly overworked hand.

When I'd discovered Libby's mom was pregnant, we hadn't been together. My beautiful baby girl was actually the product of a hot one-night stand. Mags had tracked me down when she'd been five months pregnant, and I'd shifted my life to Kirkby, where she'd lived at the time, to support her at the end of her pregnancy before taking sole custody of Libby.

"You know," Carter continued, "I could try to set you up."

I contemplated it for all of three seconds. A quick fuck was all that was on the cards for me, so being fixed up with someone who Carter knew didn't sit well. It screamed awkward. "Thanks, but I'll pass."

He raised his brow and made to speak, no doubt

to argue his case. I stopped him with a slight flick of my raised hand. "Listen, Carter, I know you mean well, but honestly, I'm good."

From his dipped brows and the twist of his lips, I didn't think he bought it. But tough. Having my best friend happy with Carter was awesome, but it didn't mean I needed that or was chasing it.

Tanner, no doubt hearing the finality of my tone, intervened. "Hey, baby, you wanna help me a minute?"

With a smile, Carter angled toward Tanner. "Lead the way, handsome."

I threw Tanner a relieved smile. "I'm just gonna slip outside for a few. Will you listen out for Libby?"

Tanner nodded as he handed me an extra beer. "Yep, no worries." I took it, grateful, and headed outside.

CONTINUE DAVIS'S STORY, I'VE GOT YOU, TODAY!

THANKS

Thanks for reading *Let Me Show You*. I do hope you enjoyed Carter and Tanner's story. I appreciate your help in spreading the word, including telling a friend. Before you go, it would mean so much to me if you would take a few minutes to write a review and share how you feel about my story so others may find my work. Reviews really do help readers find books. Please leave a review on your favourite book site.

ACKNOWLEDGMENTS

Following on from my dedication, I'm a firm believer in surrounding yourself with beautiful souls and the rest honestly falling in to place.

I'm blessed to have found my people, my family, both blood and those bonded by friendship.

My Hot Tree family (both authors and colleagues) keep me strong. Their belief in me and all we're creating makes me feel so damn privileged every single day. I thank whatever happy unicorn is watching over me every single day for the love I'm shown.

The wonderful thing about family is the ability to grow and change. With a big heart and dedicated to the belief that love truly is love, there honestly is room for more. If you've reached this far and have absorbed these words, thank you for taking the time to read my story and coming along for the ride. And above all else, welcome to my small family.

ABOUT THE AUTHOR

Becca Seymour lives and breathes all things book related. Usually with at least three books being read and two WiPs being written at the same time, life is merrily hectic. She tends to do nothing by halves so happily seeks the craziness and busyness life offers.

Living on her small property in Queensland with her human family as well as her animal family of cows, chooks, and dogs, Becca appreciates the beauty of the world around her and is a believer that love truly is love.

To check for updates head to Becca's website:
https://beccaseymour.com
You can sign up for her newsletter here:
https://mailchi.mp/4d9f2a5109b8/becca-seymour
Plus, join her Facebook group, which she shares
with the awesome Louisa Masters here:
https://www.facebook.com/
groups/seymourbookswithmasterfulmen/

facebook.com/beccaseymourauthor

twitter.com/beccaseymour_

instagram.com/authorbeccaseymour

bookbub.com/authors/becca-seymour

9 781925 853681